THE
HONYOCKER

**Center Point
Large Print**

**This Large Print Book carries the
Seal of Approval of N.A.V.H.**

ॐ श्री गणेशाय नमः

THE HONYOCKER

GILES A. LUTZ

CENTER POINT PUBLISHING
THORNDIKE, MAINE

This Center Point Large Print edition
is published in the year 2002 by arrangement with
Golden West Literary Agency.

The text of this Large Print edition is unabridged. In other
aspects, this book may vary from the original edition. Printed in
Thailand. Set in 16-point Times New Roman type by
Bill Coskrey and Gary Socquet.

ISBN 1-58547-226-3

Library of Congress Cataloging-in-Publication Data.

Lutz, Giles A.
    The honyocker / Giles A. Lutz.--Center Point large print ed.
    p. cm.
    ISBN 1-58547-226-3 (lib. bdg. : alk. paper)
    1. Large type books. I. Title.

PS3562.U83 H66 2002
813'.54--dc21

2002022260

CHAPTER ONE

This was big country, its vast reaches dwarfing the physical senses and awing the spirit. Its towering mountains buttressed the great plains, rebuffing the eye on both vertical and horizontal plane. Man was an inconsequential mote, and his feeble scratching made little impression on the great emptiness. It was a country of bitter intensities, the white winter cold of it making the marrow of a man's bones brittle and aching, its summer heat and scorching sun sucking the last drop of moisture from him, leaving him exhausted and panting.

It was early spring and too hot for this time of the year. Man tore his living from a grudging nature, and her blows were endless. Why then, did he stay here? It was a question Ashel Backus often asked himself. He yelled at the plodding team and rubbed at the sweat trickling into his eyes. He guessed the answer to his question was hope—hope that this year would be better than the last. It never happened that way. Montana held out a hope and a promise, and both were mocking lies. This year was going to be as bad as the three behind it. It was hot and dry too early in the year. The plow furrows showed enough moisture to sprout the wheat. Then the wind would tear at the tender green plants. What the wind did not tear out of the soil, the sun and heat would shrivel. It scared a man to think about a fourth successive bad year.

He yelled again at the plodding team. The house and shed were in sight, and that quickened their step more than his voice. Nellie and Lady were old and tired, in as sorry condition as the mended harness. Even the freshness of the morning could not hurry their lagging steps, and by noon they were barely moving. A good team, by working from sunup to dark, could plow three acres. Nellie and Lady could not finish two.

His broken boots raised little puffs of dust with each step. The jerking handles of a plow built arm and back muscle and strengthened shoulders. When the gain was measured against the cost, it was small return. His blue shirt was darkened with sweat, and the dried sweating showed white rimed at the armpits. His shirt and trousers were mended many times, patch being put upon patch. His face was long and angular, the eyes deep set and brooding. The features were good, cut with clean and sharp strokes. A smile or laughter could completely change his face, lighting it and building an appeal there. He rarely found cause for either expression. His hair was black and long, covering the upper rim of his ears and reaching down his neck, where it curled at the nape. A town haircut was a priceless luxury, and he would not let either of his older brothers cut it again, not after the butchering they did on it last time. He lacked an inch of being six feet, but his leanness and the lift of his head gave him the appearance of being taller. He looked ten years older than his twenty years, the youth too soon sucked and pounded out of him.

Paw Backus came out of the house as Ashel approached it. Calling the structure a house was being kind to it. It stood shadeless, a single room twelve by sixteen feet. It had a gable roof, a window in each end and a door in the middle of the east side. It sat flat on the ground without foundation. The exterior was tar paper over siding, and the years of wind had worried and torn at it until strips of bare boards showed. Tattered edges of the tar paper flapped in any breeze, and the sound of it always put a tight look around his eyes.

Paw was shorter than any of his sons, shrunken in flesh and spirit. Ordinarily his eyes were vague. But they could fire when he talked about what he was going to do next year. Always it was next year. He complained of terrible pains in his belly, pains that kept him from doing the work he wanted to do. Maybe he was sickly. One man could never know for sure how another one felt. But eating never bothered those belly pains. Paw could outdo anyone at the table.

"You're in awful early," Paw said.

"Look at these damned reins. They broke on me four times today." He held out the reins for Paw's inspection. They looked to be made of as much wire as leather. Each time they broke, Ashel poked a hole beyond each broken edge, then looped a short length of wire through the holes, drawing the edges together before he twisted the wire. "They're beyond any more repair. We need new ones."

The tragic look came to Paw's face. It always did at the mention of something needed to buy. "Don't know where we'll get the money. Everything goes out and nothing comes in."

"I'm going into town and see if I can talk Ramsey into crediting us for a new set."

Paw's face brightened. "That'll be fine, Ashel. We can get on with the plowing tomorrow. You tell Ramsey the crops look fine. Tell him he'll get all his money right after harvest. Tell him—"

Ashel cut him short. "Ramsey knows what's going on around here."

By "we getting on with the plowing" Paw meant Ashel, and Ashel was sick of doing most of it. "Hobe and Nobby will do the plowing tomorrow. They said they'd be out to take over this afternoon. Why weren't they?"

Something evasive showed in his father's face, and Ashel seized his shoulder. "Where are they now?"

"I don't know. They said they had something to do."

Ashel's fingers bit deeper, and Paw yelled, "You let go of me. Who do you think you are—"

"You'd better tell me," Ashel said grimly.

Paw swallowed hard. "They went hunting. You know we need fresh meat."

"Where?"

Paw's jaw set with a familiar stubbornness. "I don't know."

Ashel let go of his shoulder. He still thought Paw had guilty knowledge, but he was not going to get it out of him. It all depended upon what Hobe and Nobby were hunting. Elk, venison—or beef. Some of the homesteaders were helping themselves to an occasional steer. They took a grave risk. Already the ranchers were angry. A few more incidents could blow the lid off their tempers.

He unhitched the team and led them into the rickety shed. He stripped the harness from them and measured out a dab of oats, noting how low the grain was in the bin. They would have to buy more and soon, for horses needed grain while they were in heavy work.

He said, "They'd better stay off of Vaughan's land—or any other rancher's."

"Why?" Paw cried. "The ranchers got so much, and we've got so little. It don't seem fair—" He stopped before Ashel's accusing eyes, then said weakly, "I wouldn't let Hobe or Nobby go over there."

Ashel thought that Paw was lying. But Hobe and Nobby were on foot. They would be unable to pack game—or beef—very far. They might be able to pick up a couple of sage hens or a rabbit but probably nothing more. He stepped outside the shed and looked toward Vaughan's land. The M swinging V lay the closest of any of the cattlemen's land. If Hobe and Nobby were over there, finding them in that vast expanse would be an impossible job. "They better be smart enough to stay where they belong."

"Everybody is against us," Paw said. "Everybody lied to us. It was better in Missouri."

Paw was right in one of his statements, wrong in the other. At least, the railroad lied. Their lying brochure was still somewhere in the house. It spoke of a new, rich land with ample water. One hundred and sixty acres for the man who had foresight to make the move. And so they came. Families from Wisconsin and Minnesota, from Iowa and Missouri. They were met with hostility from the cow- and sheepman, for each new plow meant that so much grass was forever lost. They were cheated when they bought materials and supplies. They were abused and derided, the Montanans calling them Honyockers, lumping all races and origins in the one contemptuous term. The Slavic people, from Minnesota, were the first arrivals and were called Hunyaks. Ashel supposed Honyocker derived from that. Paw was right about people being against them, about people lying to them. But he was wrong about it being better in Missouri. Ashel remembered the sour, thin soil of the Ozarks. It grew corn no higher than a man's waist with nubbins that were barely longer than his middle finger. All the grinding toil in the world produced no more than a bare living from that land.

He said flatly, "Maybe it wasn't any worse, but it wasn't any better."

He walked toward the house, leaving Paw talking to himself. The interior walls of the house were pasted up with old rotogravure sections for wall covering. He knew every picture there. His mother liked to look at them. A thousand times he had heard her sigh and say, "My, they're pretty."

A sagging bed was at the far end of the room, curtained off with muslin. That was his parents' private space. The stools and tables were made of boxes, and above the cast-iron cook stove were curtained shelves for cupboards. The floor was warped and cracked, and the doors and windows did not hang. In the winter, they stuffed rags into the widening cracks.

He said, "Maw, I'm going into town. Is there anything you want?"

She sat before the stove, peeling potatoes for the evening meal. Her lank, colorless hair hung down the sides of her face. Her face was dispirited, her shoulders slumped. She was twenty years younger than she looked, and he felt a sense of outrage as he looked at her. Could there ever have been youth and life in her face?

She thought a moment, then sighed. "I guess not." There were many things she wanted, but the years of privation clamped their iron discipline about her. It was best not to think of the wanted things. A body did not hurt so much that way.

She said, "You're going to wait for supper?"

He shook his head. "I'm not hungry, Maw."

He had a dollar in his pocket, a dollar that none of them knew about. Maybe he ought to buy her something, a hair ribbon or a skirt. He thought about it, finding pleasure in it. She would fuss about it, saying they needed so many other things, but her eyes would glow.

She said, "Ashel, see if you can call Elodia into the house. She can finish these potatoes."

He stepped to the door and called to his twelve-year-old sister.

Elodia burst into the room like a young tornado. She was as flat bodied as a boy and leggy as a new colt.

"Elodia," her mother cried. "How many times do I have to tell you to quit running in the house. You sit down here and finish these potatoes."

Elodia made a face, but she obeyed.

Ashel grinned at her, then his face sobered. The very young were lucky. They accepted things as they were, without fuss or strain. The added years would bring their discontent. He wished he could keep it from her. Maybe he could stretch his dollar to include a few pennies' worth of candy for her.

He walked toward the box in which he kept his clothes. He had one shirt there, patched but clean. He wished he could do more about his appearance. Someday, he thought fiercely, he would. Someday he would ride into town and not be ashamed of how he looked.

Elodia watched him put on the shirt. "Where are you going, Ashel?"

"Town."

"I wish I could go into town with you," she said wistfully. "I don't like it when you're not here. Hobe and Nobby tease me."

He finished buttoning the shirt and said, "Maw, make them let her alone."

His mother said with a flare of spirit, "Haven't I enough to do without keeping all of you from fighting? She's big enough to take care of herself."

Ashel ran his hand over the child's head. "Stay away from them," he advised.

He went back out to the shed, and Paw was still there. "You going to miss supper?" Paw asked.

Ashel nodded as he slipped the bit into Lady's mouth. Lady was younger than Nellie and a shade more lively. He would have to ride her bareback. He hated to have to go into town like that, for he saw derision in the eyes of every cowman he passed.

Paw shook his head as though someone choosing to miss a meal was beyond comprehension. "Talk to Ramsey real good, Ashel. We've got to have those reins."

Ashel led Lady out of the shed, grabbed her mane, and swung up onto her back. "You tell Hobe and Nobby they're going to plow tomorrow. I'm not."

He kicked Lady with his heels and jogged down the lane leading to the road that ran toward town. He would get up early enough in the morning to be sure Hobe and Nobby did not slip away. Work was the only thing that was going to lift this family, but he would be damned if he'd do it all.

He let Lady pick her own pace, knowing it was useless to yell and pound at her. On both sides of the road, as far as he could see, was turned land. A lot of the homesteaders had already finished their plowing. He put in as many hours as any of them and did not accomplish nearly as much. Better teams and better equipment were the answer. But how was he going to get those things until they made a decent crop? It was a spine-studded question, pricking him from whichever angle he approached it.

He passed Greeble's place and waved to him without stopping. Greeble was a talker, and Ashel was in no mood for it. Greeble's house had clapboard siding instead of tar paper. It made a much better appearance, and Ashel wanted that, wanted it for himself and his family.

The four miles to town was a long, slow ride. Ekalaka was an ugly town without a tree or bush to break the lines of its ugliness. It was a shack town, its houses and buildings constructed with only utility in mind. The business section ran for three blocks, and the main street was dry and dusty and still showing deep ruts from last winter's moisture. In the winter and spring, a team could hardly pull through the muddy street. In the summer, the dust choked them. The stores were drab little buildings with dirty showcases. Most of the goods they handled were third-rate, but they charged first-rate prices for them. A man could get a soft drink without charged water or eat a poor meal in the one restaurant. Or he could buy whisky in one of the two saloons. Other than those things, Ekalaka had little to offer in the way of diversion.

He tied Lady at the edge of town, not wanting to ride her bareback through the street and advertise his poverty.

He stopped at Emerson's store first. His dollar did not go very far. It bought a shirtwaist for his mother and a nickel's worth of hard candy for Elodia. The shirtwaist was of cheap material and a few washings would dull it, but right now it was new and bright.

Emerson never spoke to him during the entire transaction, and Ashel felt the heat in his face. Emerson would not speak to him, but he would take his money readily enough.

He left the store and turned toward Ramsey's saddle and harness shop. Two cowmen galloped past him, and Ashel turned his head, following their course. Emerson would welcome their trade; he would not treat them with contemptuous silence.

He walked the twenty yards to Ramsey's place and stepped inside. It smelled of new and old leather and of dust. Every store in Ekalaka had that same dusty smell.

Ramsey had the same cold, weighing look in his eyes. He was a short, fat man with pouched eyes. His hands were thick and stubby, the fingers calloused from long hours of working leather. He was good at it. Ashel kept his eyes off the display of saddles. He knew what they cost.

He said, "I need a new set of reins."

"You got the money to pay for them?"

"No."

Color darkened Ramsey's face, and his angry words ran over each other. "Did you expect to walk in here and charge them? Do you know how much your bill is now?"

"I know." Ashel stared steadily at him. "If I don't get the reins, there won't be any crop. You won't get any of your money then."

"Oh, goddamn it." Ramsey's hands lifted and fell in a helpless gesture. "I've got a secondhand pair I can let you have."

Ashel followed him to the rear of the store and inspected the reins. They were still in serviceable condition. His lips tightened at the price Ramsey quoted. The price was not too far under that of a new set.

He said, "All right." He had to take them, and Ramsey had to let him have them. Both of them were caught in a vicious squeeze of protecting what was already invested.

He folded the reins several times and slung them over his shoulder. He wished he could pay the damned bill in full. He needed the self-respect it would build. He said, "One of these days things will be different." Maybe for once Paw could be right. Maybe this *was* their year. One decent crop could do so much for them.

Ramsey growled, "I hope so. If it isn't, you Honyockers are going to break me."

Ashel left before he said something unwise. Ramsey had so little regard for him he made no attempt to veil his contempt. It was a galling thing for a man to take naked contempt and make no return.

He walked toward Lady, wanting to get out of town as quickly as possible. Something hot and wicked felt as though it were crawling just beneath his skin. If he looked at any more hatred or contempt, that hot, wicked crawling would explode into the open.

He crossed the side street that ran beside the livery stable's corral, and a girl's voice carried to him from the end of the corral. "Let me pass," she said.

The voice was familiar and he turned his head. Two cowmen had a girl penned in against the corral's fence. Every time she tried to move, one of them stepped in front of her, blocking her passage. Ashel caught a glimpse of her face between the shoulders of the two men. Cassandra Reynolds' face was grave but not frightened.

Ashel started for the little group, both hands squeezing the folded-up reins. He heard the bigger of the two men say, "Honey, what's your hurry? Have you been around those Honyockers so long you can't recognize a real man?"

She caught sight of Ashel and said, "You'd better let me go, Mister Cabe."

She had more confidence in Ashel than he had in himself. He knew Dandy Cabe by sight. Cabe was Milo Vaughan's foreman. Ashel supposed the other man was an M swinging V hand. Both of them were armed. Ashel had only the folded-up reins and his hands. He felt downright uneasy.

She looked past them to Ashel. She was eighteen and pretty. A few more years would wipe out the immaturity in her face, and the prettiness would change to beauty. She considered herself Ashel's girl, though no promise had passed between them. He would not let himself consider beyond the immediate fact of knowing her. The home-steaders' wives too soon became dried up and lifeless. The picture of his mother flashed into his mind. He would not do that to Cassie. He would not expect her to live in a shack and make do with nothing. And until he could offer more— He let the thought beat itself to pieces against the blank wall it always ran up against.

Cabe was too absorbed in his baiting of Cassie to hear Ashel's approach. "Why, honey," he said. "You wouldn't run off and leave me, would you?" He reached out to put a hand on her shoulder.

The fear was great enough in Ashel to knot in his

stomach. He took two more steps and said, "Take your hand off her, Cabe."

The looped reins dangled from his hands. If he got a sufficient swing he could smash Cabe across the face with enough force to stagger him at least. What came beyond that he did not dare think about.

The two men whirled to face him, and astonishment froze their faces. Cabe recovered first and laughed. The laugh had an ugly sound.

"Well, look who's giving us orders, Pete."

Cassie tried to slip past Cabe, and he threw out an arm, blocking her. "You stay here, honey. You're going to enjoy seeing this."

He was in his middle thirties and powerfully built through the chest and shoulders. Coarse blond hair showed under the shoved-back hat, and his eyes were a pale blue. His chin was as harsh as a jutting cliff, and a stamp of brutality was in the thin line of the lips. His clothing was new and fancy, and he wore a red silk neckerchief knotted about his throat. He was almost a head taller than Ashel and perhaps twenty pounds heavier.

Pete was a small, dark man, and his manner showed he was in the habit of taking orders from Cabe. He grinned, his teeth flashing in his dark face. "You suppose we oughta apologize to the Honyocker, Dandy?"

Cabe laughed again, and the sound scraped across Ashel's tightened nerves. "We'll have to apologize to the pieces, because I'm going to take him apart."

Cassie's face was white, and her mouth was an O. She was scared, too, scared for Ashel.

She lifted her head and stared toward the intersection.

"Paw," she called. "I'm down here."

Ashel turned his head. Clell Reynolds was standing on the corner, talking to two men. He jerked his head around at Cassie's call, stared for a moment, than started toward them, the two men following him. Ashel recognized them, then—Abe Milton and Suge Thomas.

Cabe saw them coming, and his lips went tight with suppressed fury.

Ashel said, "You'd better let it drop here, Cabe."

Cabe cursed him in a low, venomous tone. "I don't know your name, Honyocker, but I've seen you around before. And I'll see you again." He made the words a promise—a promise to himself and Ashel Backus. "Come on, Pete," he said.

He stalked past Ashel, Pete at his heels. He was not leaving because of fear of the suddenly shifted odds. Ashel was wise enough to know that. But this was happening in town, and it could mean interference from other sources and even greater odds. Dandy Cabe was content to wait to carry out his promise.

His shoulder brushed Reynolds' as he passed the three men. Neither man was giving an inch to the other. Cassie stepped up beside Ashel and seized his hand. He felt the warm pressure and the tremble in the fingers. "Don't say anything to Paw," she warned.

Ashel nodded as Reynolds approached.

Reynolds was a short, blocky man with a square-cut, almost harsh face. His shoulders were work stooped, and he had the blunt, square hands of a plowman. His gray eyes were smoldering. Cassie got the color of her eyes from him.

He asked, "Was he bothering Cassie, Ashel?"

Ashel shook his head. "We were just talking about the weather."

"With a cowman?" Reynolds said incredulously. "Cassie, was he bothering you?"

"No," she said, and Ashel thought the denial came too quickly to smooth Reynolds' suspicions.

"Cassie, don't lie to me," he snapped. "If he was bothering you, he can be stopped. We've got rights, even though they don't think we have."

"There was no trouble, Clell," Ashel said calmly.

"It looked like trouble to me," Suge Thomas said stubbornly, and Milton nodded agreement.

Ashel saw the same look in all three faces. They wanted an excuse from him so that they could push this. All the past abuses, real and fancied, were rankling.

Reynolds' eyes turned unfriendly. "You're covering up something," he accused. "You sound to me like you're siding with them."

"Paw," Cassie cried in protest.

"Well, he does," Reynolds said doggedly. "They burned Tom Ackerman's barn down a couple of nights ago. He's talking of selling out. They've driven him out of the country. And you're protecting someone like that."

Heat was in Ashel's face, but he kept his voice even. "Do you know Cabe was behind the burning?"

Reynolds shook his head.

"But you're ready enough to accuse him for it."

Reynolds' face turned a dark red at the rebuke. "I'm beginning to see where you might be standing."

"You don't see a damned thing," Ashel snapped.

Reynolds glared at him. "There's no use trying to talk to you. Come on, Cassie."

"In a minute, Paw. I want to talk to Ashel."

She waited until the three moved away, then said, "Don't be angry with him, Ashel."

Ashel ruefully grinned. "I'd say it was the other way around. Clell wanted trouble. He was actually looking for it. And he's sore because we wouldn't give him an excuse."

"It's because they're worried, Ashel. Don't you see? Ackerman isn't the first to be hurt. And he won't be the last. Paw and the others want to strike back. At any of them."

"Even if they hit back at the wrong man," Ashel said. "Then that man will strike back at someone else. It's blind and stupid, Cassie. And the trouble will keep getting deeper until it swallows all of us."

"Cassie," Reynolds yelled. "Are you coming?"

"Right now," she called. She squeezed Ashel's hand again. "Come over in a day or two. Paw will be over his mad by then."

Ashel doubted it. He remembered the unfriendly light in Reynolds' eyes. "We'll see, Cassie," he said, and it was no promise.

He watched Cassie join the three men. A few more incidents from either side were all that was needed. Then they would start a fire that no one could stomp out.

CHAPTER TWO

It was dark when he returned home. The glow of the kerosene lamp in the window was a beacon, beckoning to him from a mile away. The countryside was dotted with such beacons many more than three years ago. But there were black, empty spaces, where some lights had shone last year. Some of the homesteaders were quitting, leaving this country with less than they came in with. He had seen them pass the house, their wagons loaded with every material thing they possessed. It was sad to see them go, beaten and dispirited with the waste of the years and the toil going for nothing.

He stared angrily at the black sky, ablaze with its stars. It looked warm and friendly, but he knew differently. It was a part of nature, and man fought an unequal war with her. He shook his head and prodded Lady with his heels, wanting to get home.

Paw heard the sound of the hoofs and came to the door. "That you, Ashel?" he called.

"Yes," Ashel answered and rode on toward the shed. He heard Lady's weary sigh as he stripped the bridle from her. He slapped her rump and walked out of the shed.

Paw came toward him, and there was an anxious note in his voice as he asked, "What did Ramsay say about the reins?"

"I got them. They're in the shed."

Paw let out a relieved sigh. "Now you can get at the plowing tomorrow."

"Not me," Ashel said. Paw only remembered what he wanted to. "Hobe and Nobby. What time did they get in?"

Paw hesitated too long, and Ashel asked sharply, "Are they still out?"

Paw muttered, "Yes. I'm looking for them any minute, now."

Ashel caught his worry and said, "You'd better worry if they went after Vaughan's beef." He started to tell Paw about the incident in town, then thought better of it. But both sides were drawing farther apart. And both sides were looking for blame to put upon the other. They'll find it, he thought. When a man looked hard enough for anything, he found it.

"I want to talk to them when they come in." If he could help it, none of the Backus family was going to give additional reason to put blame upon the homesteaders.

He went into the house and gave his mother the shirt-waist. He was rewarded by the shine in her eyes. The shine did not last too long. Worry crept in and pushed it to one side. "Didn't it cost an awful lot, Ashel?"

Elodia tugged on his arm. "Didn't you bring me anything, Ashel?"

He pulled the little sack of candy from his pocket. The same kind of a shine was in her eyes, only she added audible sound to her pleasure, a sort of little croon.

From the doorway Paw said sourly, "You're throwing money around like we're rich."

Ashel held back his hot retort. Paw was talking about a dollar, a lone, measly dollar. His own dollar, at that. It might have bought something the family needed more, but he did not give a damn. He was tired of practicality holding his nose to the grindstone.

"It didn't cost very much," he assured his mother.

She gave him a grateful smile, just a little weary around the edges. "Are you hungry?" she asked.

He discovered he was. She made him a sandwich out of tired, cold side meat. A few bites and his hunger left him.

The tiny cellar, beneath the trap door in the floor, was doing a poor job of refrigeration.

Elodia was watching him, and she said, "It isn't very good, is it?" She glanced defiantly at her father. "Paw got mad at me when I said that at supper."

An angry wash of color spread across Paw's face. He and Elodia must have had quite a few words about that meat. "Don't blame me," Paw yelled. "I told him we needed fresh meat."

Ashel could not dispute that. But they could not steal it. The moral side was the least important. They could not steal it because of the actual danger to them.

He picked up his pallet and walked outside. With that many people sleeping in the single room, the air grew rank. He slept outdoors every time the weather permitted it. So did Hobe and Nobby. He would hear them when they came in, and he would have that talk with them. He fell asleep with the thought in mind.

He thought he heard them come in during the night, but he was too sleepy to do more than mumble a few words. The east sun awakened him in the morning. He yawned and stretched, savoring the few delicious moments before getting up. He yawned again, then turned his head. He did not dream he heard Hobe and Nobby come in last night, for their pallets were a dozen yards from him. But they were gone. He frowned at the empty pallets. Hobe and Nobby usually had to be called in the morning.

He walked to the water bucket and was not surprised to find it empty. He drew a fresh bucket and filled the pan. He washed his face and upper body, lavishly sloshing water onto himself with cupped hands.

Paw came around the corner of the house, yawning and scratching himself. He said, "Ashel, that's an awful waste of water. Washing like that." He drew no reply, and his tone turned fretful. "You know the well went dry last summer."

Ashel knew it. How could he forget those long hours of hauling water? But saving a third of a bucketful now would not prevent the well from going dry a month or two later.

He must have slept later than he thought, for everyone seemed to be up before him. Paw was another one that was hard to get out of bed.

He asked, "Where's Hobe and Nobby?"

That curious, evasive quality was in Paw's eyes again. "They're down at the shed. You can talk to them at breakfast."

Ashel frowned. Paw was hiding something and doing a poor job of it.

"I'll talk to them now." He walked toward the shed, Paw tagging at his heels and arguing against it with every step.

Hobe and Nobby were not in the shed. Neither was Nellie. Ashel did not have to look to see if the plow was there, for that would be ridiculous. Hobe and Nobby never started this early in their life.

He turned suddenly and slammed the heel of his palm against his father's shoulder. It knocked Paw into the shed wall. He opened his mouth to yell his protest, and the look on Ashel's face left his mouth open with no sound coming out of it.

"Now, you tell me where they are and what they're doing." He drew back his hand. "And none of your damned lying."

The look on his face crumpled the last of Paw's resistance. He would not meet Ashel's eyes as he talked.

"They were just hunting around yesterday. They found a steer with a busted leg. They left him that way, figuring he'd keep better. They took knives with them this morning. They're going to butcher that steer this morning and bring in as much meat as Nellie can carry."

"Whose steer was it?"

"Milo Vaughan's," Paw said sullenly.

Ashel remembered the look on Cabe's face yesterday evening. This would give him an excuse to do anything he wanted to any member of the Backus family. "The crazy fools," he exploded. "And you let them go. If Vaughan catches them on his land, do you know what he will do to them?"

"He won't catch them. Hobe and Nobby are too smart for that."

Ashel ran toward the house. His mother was cooking oatmeal, and she said, "It's not ready yet."

Ashel looked at the rifle pegs. The good rifle was gone. The one left had a defective firing pin. It misfired as often as not.

He took it down from its pegs and went back outside.

Paw asked, "Where are you going?"

"I'm going to try to catch them. How long ago did they leave?"

The sullen look was back on Paw's face. "Maybe an hour ago."

It gave them quite a lead. But Nellie was slow, and she was carrying double. That would help cut some off that lead.

Paw grabbed at his arm. "Its leg was busted, Ashel. It

won't do anybody any good, just laying out there. We need the meat. Vaughan would only shoot it, if he found it."

Ashel knocked the hand away. What Paw said was probably true. But if Vaughan found Hobe and Nobby butchering the steer, he would also probably hang them.

"You want them hanged?" he demanded.

That scared Paw. He swallowed and said, "Maybe you'd better go after them."

"I intend to."

He walked to the shed and put a bridle on Lady. He led her outside and jumped onto her back. He did not look at his father as he turned Lady toward the nearest M swinging V land.

It was not hard to track Nellie across the plowed land. She was a heavy animal and with the double weight on her back, her hoofs sank deep. He crossed Hoffer's land, then Simmons', and the trail was as plain as marks on a paper. But the plowed land ran out after a mile or so. He rode over grass country, and it was harder to trail Nellie. The grass was springy and resilient, and he had to look closely to see an occasional imprint of crushed grass. As he searched, he wondered about the grass. Its new greenness seemed sturdy enough. It would go on and grow when the wheat was shriveling. Why was that? He did not know, unless the new grass formed a sod and the old grass a mulch, the two things working together to hold what little moisture the land received.

He lost the trail and spent several minutes trying to pick it up. He could cast about in ever-growing circles, until he cut it again, but he decided the quickest course was to get to Vaughan's fence as quickly as possible. Hobe and

Nobby crossed it someplace, and there had to be evidence of their crossing.

He reached Vaughan's fence and stopped. He looked in both directions, and to the limit of his vision he could see no gate or break in the four strands of barb-wire. It was only a guess which direction to go, and he chose south.

He rode almost a mile before he found the place where his brothers crossed the fence. The staples were out of four posts, and the strands of wire were pressed to the ground and held there by a large rock. He felt something go tight in him as he stepped Lady across the held-down wire.

He admitted he was scared. He had no right on this land, and he wanted to find his brothers and get off of it as quickly as possible.

Anxiety was forming a lump in his throat, when he saw a fresh scuff in the earth. It was made by a hoof, and so far he was on the right trail. The country grew rougher, chopped up by breaks and washes. The rock outcropped at the surface, and he kept seeing those scuffs. Nellie never did pick up her feet well, and he knew her forehoofs were striking those outcroppings and scarring the dirt around them.

He crested a small rise and breathed a sigh of relief. Nellie stood at the edge of a break, not a quarter of a mile ahead of him. He started to halloo, then checked it. Sound carried in this emptiness. Someone besides his brothers might hear him.

When he was an eighth of a mile from Nellie, the sound of voices stopped him short. They were loud, heated voices, and they did not belong to either Hobe or Nobby. The men were apparently down in the break, for he could not see them.

He slid to the ground and carefully crawled to the edge of the break. It was some twenty feet deep and half again as wide. It twisted on a west-to-east course, and Hobe and Nobby were in it. They were backed against the north wall, and their faces were scared. Two men on horseback held them rooted. One of the men held a rifle, the other a pistol. A dead steer lay near the south side of the break, the hide half stripped from it. Hobe's and Nobby's clothing was bloodstained. They had been surprised in the middle of their work.

There was two years' difference in their ages, though they looked enough alike to be twins. Hobe was the oldest, five years older than Ashel. They were lean men with sunken cheeks and a bright, sly quality to their eyes. Usually they were reckless and assured. They were not now. Nobby's mouth hung slack, and Hobe's lips moved without being able to make a sound.

"You goddamned cow thieves," the older rider said. "We caught you in the act. What will we do with them. Lanny?" His shoulders were thin and stooped, and his face showed the wear of weather and time.

Lanny grinned, showing strong, white teeth. His head was erect with the cockiness of youth. He pointed the rifle at Nobby, and Nobby cowered.

"It's a good thing I heard that shot," Lanny said. "They were so interested in their work they didn't hear us ride up. What do you want to do with them, Tom?"

Tom scowled and holstered his pistol. He unlimbered his rope and shook out a loop. "Hanging's too good for them."

Hobe's face went even whiter under the dirt. "Wait." He

threw out a pleading hand. "We shot the steer. I admit it. But we found him down here with a broken leg. It wouldn't do nobody any good laying here."

"You probably drove him over," Tom said coldly. "If your story's true, it don't excuse a thing. You got no business on M swinging V land. Maybe a little dragging will teach you that."

Lanny whooped. "That's it, Tom. We'll drag the clothes off them, then their hides. They'll think a long time before they cross our fence again."

CHAPTER THREE

Ashel drew a deep breath and stood. He had to rely upon a defective rifle, but they did not know that. It would not take much dragging to injure a man seriously—or even kill him. "Hold it," he said.

All heads jerked toward him. "Drop those guns," he ordered.

Hobe's face went loose with his relief. "Ashel," he said weakly.

Ashel made a movement with the rifle muzzle. "I meant it." He locked eyes with the riders, and they were convinced.

Tom pulled his rifle from its scabbard and dropped it. He drew his pistol from its holster, and it followed the rifle.

"You," Ashel ordered, jerking the rifle toward Lanny.

Lanny swore as he let both weapons fall to the ground.

"Pick up those guns," Ashel told Hobe and Nobby. "And climb out of there."

Lanny watched him with ugly eyes. "This isn't over,

Honyocker."

Nobby held a rifle and a pistol, and his face was mean. It was a familiar expression to Ashel. Every time Nobby drew a bead on something, even a rabbit, his eyes seemed to turn red. While neither gun was actually leveled at the two riders, Ashel knew that in his mind's eye Nobby was looking at them over gun sights.

"Nobby," he said sharply.

It broke Nobby's attention, and Nobby's eyes swiveled toward him. "I said climb out of there."

Nobby started climbing, and Hobe followed him. When they reached the top, Ashel said, "Give me those guns." He would not breathe easy until he had every gun. That red look was still in Nobby's eyes.

Hobe was reluctant to hand over the guns he carried. "We ought to kill the sons of bitches," he said. A moment ago he had been a groveling, frightened creature. Now he talked about murder.

"You've caused enough trouble," Ashel said savagely. He jerked the guns from Hobe's hands. His rage broke at the stubbornness remaining in Nobby's face, and he pointed a pistol at him. "I'll shoot you as quick as I would them."

His ferocity washed over Nobby. "Have you gone crazy?" he asked, his eyes round. But as he spoke, he handed over the weapons to Ashel.

Ashel stuck the pistols in his waistband. He had four rifles to carry, and it made quite a burden.

"You two get on Nellie and ride out of here," he commanded. He knew this was not over. The two riders sitting below him were smarting under this handling. They had right on their side. The half-skinned steer was proof of it. They would collect for these minutes and collect hard. All they had to do was to tell Cabe, describe Ashel, and Cabe would recognize him as the one who affronted him in town. Cabe would have a double reason to find him, and knowing the man, one was enough. This matter went beyond just Ashel. Now the entire family was involved.

He waited until Nellie was moving, then looked at the two men below him. "You'll find your guns at the fence. Don't come after them right away."

Lanny cursed him with a savagery that brought color to Ashel's face.

Tom said, "It's all right, Lanny. We'll get our day."

Words were on Ashel's tongue, but he forced them back. He knew how far he would get trying to reason with either of them.

As he walked to where Lady stood, he kept turning his head to watch the edge of the break. They must have been convinced he meant what he said, for he caught no glimpse of them.

It was awkward mounting Lady with his burden of weapons. He kicked her into a lope and caught up with Hobe and Nobby. "You crazy fools," he said passionately.

"There wasn't any use letting that meat go to waste." Hobe would not look at Ashel.

"Did you drive it over the edge?"

"We did not. Did we, Nobby?"

Nobby backed him up too quickly, and Ashel thought, They're lying. He said, "I think you spent most of yesterday afternoon trying to stampede cattle into that break. You finally got a steer over." It would be slow, tedious work for men on foot, but if they were determined enough, they could succeed. Cattle would only run so far before they settled down again, and a couple of men by pushing at them could force them in the direction they wanted.

"Think what you want to," Hobe said sullenly, and his expression told Ashel he was somewhere near the truth.

He said, "They won't let it drop. They'll be coming after us. It may take a little time, but they'll find us."

"Let 'em," Nobby said. "With all those guns you got, we'll blow them out of their saddles."

Ashel cursed him; he cursed Nobby as savagely as Lanny had cursed him. "Let them come," he repeated bitterly. "There's only Maw and Elodia at home. Let them burn down the shed, then the house."

That reached Nobby, for his voice lost its belligerence. "What are we going to do?"

Ashel shook his head. "I don't know." A thought was forming in his head. He did not want it there, but he could not keep it out. If he could reach Milo Vaughan and talk to him before Lanny and Tom did, there might be a chance of squaring this. He had to try, and the thought left him greasy with fear.

He stepped Lady over the wires at the fence and stopped her. Hobe and Nobby would have ridden on, and he checked them. "Put those wires back up."

Hobe had the staples in his pocket, and Ashel watched him pound them back with a rock. He leaned over and dropped two rifles and the pistols at the foot of one of the posts. He had one good rifle left and the one with the defective firing pin. If the M swinging V rode against them in force, the Backus family was poorly equipped to stop them.

"You're crazy to leave those guns there," Hobe muttered. He reddened under Ashel's angry eyes. "You been acting pretty big this morning. Maybe we can change that."

He took a step toward Ashel, and Ashel said, "You come any farther, and I'll break your head with a rifle barrel."

Hobe weighed Ashel, and his eyes turned malevolent. "It can wait," he said and moved toward Nellie.

Things were going fine, Ashel thought. He had the M swinging V outfit against him on one side and his family on the other.

He trailed behind his brothers all the way to the house. Paw saw them coming and hurried to the shed to meet them. "What happened?" he cried.

"The damned fools killed one of Vaughan's steers," Ashel said. "Two of his riders caught them butchering it."

Paw had sense enough to be frightened. "They'll be coming after us," he said, and his voice trembled.

He was scared now. He should have been scared before he let Hobe and Nobby go. "What'll we do, Ashel?" he asked.

"I'm going to see Vaughan and try to square it."

Paw looked at him big-eyed. "He might not listen to you."

Ashel knew that. Just the thought of it put a knot in his stomach. "I've got to try. How much money do we have?"

Their combined pockets yielded a total of less than three dollars. It would not go far toward buying a steer.

He clambered on Lady, and Paw came over and laid a hand on his knee. "Tell him we'll pay it off as quick as we can, Ashel. Oh, God. If they come over here, they'll wreck everything we own."

Ashel nodded. It was a little late for Paw to be thinking the way he was.

He rode out to the main road and turned north. He had never been to Vaughan's house, but he knew the general direction in which it lay. He would pass Cassie's house on the way, and he hoped neither she nor Reynolds would see him go by.

His hopes were in vain. Reynolds was out in front of the house, and he beckoned Ashel toward him with an imperious motion of his hand.

"Climb down," he said, and the gruffness in his tone was an attempt to cover his effort at making peace. "Cassie's putting something to eat on the table."

Ashel shook his bead. "I can't, Clell. I've got something to do."

Suspicion immediately changed Reynolds' face. "What? There's nothing in the direction you're going but Milo Vaughan."

Ashel nodded, saying nothing. He could explain to Reynolds, but a pride held back the words. A man did not say, "My brothers are thieves," he thought fiercely. Besides it's none of his business.

"You're going to see Vaughan." Reynolds made it a statement. "What kind of dealings you got with him?"

The situation rasped Ashel's nerves, and he said curtly, "My business, Clell."

Reynolds' face darkened. "It's all of our business. You pick your side, and you stay on it." He stared hard at Ashel. "I thought you and Cassie were lying last night about Cabe. Now I know it. Why were you protecting him?"

Ashel's temper rose. "I wasn't protecting him," he snapped. "A man can have as much trouble as he looks for. I don't see any sense in looking." He softened his voice, hoping to make Reynolds see this in a different light. "All of us could have probably whipped Cabe and Pete last night. But do you think he'd let it stop there? He'd give it back and maybe worse, and the thing would keep on building bigger and bigger until we've got war on our hands. Is that what you want, Clell?"

"If it has to come to that, it's all right with me," Reynolds said stubbornly. "There's more of us than there is of them." His voice rose in a crescendo of rage. "Ackerman left the country this morning. Driven out by them. His barn burned, his milk cow killed. He couldn't take it any longer."

"You keep saying 'them' and 'they.' Who do you mean, Clell? Put names to them."

"All of them." Reynolds made a sweeping motion with his arm. "The cattlemen."

It was too broad an indictment, even a stupid one. Honesty and fair dealing did not run in one class of men and not in another. But Ashel knew the same broad indictment would be made by some of the cattlemen, an indictment that said all homesteaders were lazy, shiftless Honyockers. In a tide like that, running from both sides, reason and sanity did not have a chance.

Reynolds stabbed his forefinger into Ashel's thigh to emphasize his words. "I'm telling you, don't have any dealings with Vaughan or any of the rest of them. You'll be painting yourself with a pretty black brush if you do."

Ashel's mouth thinned. Clell Reynolds was more fortunate than most homesteaders in the fact that his land was better and lay lower. A creek cut through the northeast corner of it, and the flats along it raised good crops of hay, long after moisture on the uplands was gone. He said, "Don't give me orders, Clell. You sold Vaughan hay last year. Now, you tell me not to have any dealings with him."

The cords in Reynolds' neck were tightening under his rage. "This year is different from last year. He won't get any more hay from me." He had the advantage in the fact he was Cassie's father, and now he used it. "You go ahead with whatever you've got in mind, and you won't be welcome here any more."

Cassie came to the door and her face lighted when she saw Ashel. "Ashel," she called. "Get down. Dinner's on the table."

Reynolds' face was harsh set with its stubbornness. Ashel shook his head at Cassie. "Can't," he said. He glanced at Reynolds. "A man does what he feels like he has to, Clell."

He lifted the reins. He was going to see Vaughan. He could see no other course. Maybe Reynolds felt he had the same right to his stand. Cassie called his name again. He did not look around.

He continued on his way, and his anger included a lot of people —Hobe and Nobby and his father. Clell Reynolds and Vaughan's two riders, Lanny and Tom. All of them as deeply involved as himself, and yet he was carrying the brunt of it. He was the one who had to see Vaughan, he was the one who would take whatever Vaughan handed him.

He stopped Lady as he reached the narrow, fenced-in lane leading to Vaughan's house. He looked down it, and his throat felt tight. He had never seen Milo Vaughan's house, knowing there was no welcome for him or his kind. A few more steps would put him back on Vaughan's land, and the lack of welcome would still exist. If Lanny and Tom had already talked to Vaughan, it could be even worse.

He kicked Lady in the flanks and started down the lane. He had gone less than five hundred yards, when he saw the buckboard coming toward him. He pulled off as tight as he could get against the left-hand fence and waited. He could hear the thump of his heart.

A man and woman were in the buckboard. The man's head lifted as he saw Ashel, and his arms went rigid as he pulled in the team. He stopped beside Ashel, and his voice was edged as he asked, "What do you want?" The hostility in his manner said "What are you doing on my land?"

"Are you Mr. Vaughan?"

The big man nodded. "I'm Vaughan." He was barrel chested and heavy in the arms and hands. He was ruddy complexioned, and his eyes were blue, an unfriendly blue. The woman beside him was sweet faced and amply fleshed. Her face was sober at the moment, but her mouth was cut for laughter. Her brown eyes were curious as she looked at Ashel but not unfriendly.

Ashel swallowed and plunged into his story. He saw Vaughan's face grow darker. The woman placed a hand on Vaughan's forearm. Vaughan looked as though he did not feel it.

Ashel left out nothing. "They were going to drag my brothers. I took your men's guns. I left them beside the fence."

Vaughan looked as though he were going to explode.

"Now, Milo," the woman said.

"You stay out of this, Millie," he ordered. He glared at Ashel. "After your brothers killed one of my steers, you've got the gall to ride here and tell me about it."

Ashel said doggedly, "They claimed they found it with a broken leg."

"Am I supposed to believe that? Do you?"

"They're my brothers, Mr. Vaughan," Ashel said simply.

A grudging admiration crept into Vaughan's eyes. "You've got guts of a kind to come here—or gall. I don't know which. What's in your mind?"

"I want to pay for that steer."

"Can you?" It was a brutal challenge, taking in Ashel's appearance and the looks of the horse he rode.

Ashel pulled out the coins he collected from his father and brothers. They did not cover the palm of his hand. "This is all the money we have."

The angry color came back to Vaughan's face. "You're going to pay for a forty-dollar steer with that?"

"I can work it out. I'll do anything you say."

Millie said, "Milo. Listen to me." She put her lips close to his ear.

Ashel could hear only the murmur of her voice.

Vaughan grudgingly nodded. He looked at Ashel and said, "I always claimed I was fair enough to give a man a chance. I pay my men forty dollars a month. You can work a month and pay out that steer." His voice took on an edge. "You'll work. Understand that. Be here in the morning."

He lifted the reins and snapped them against the team's rumps. As the buckboard started to move Ashel heard him say, "He's your man, Millie. I want him used."

She turned her head and gave Ashel a smile. The smile said that everything was going to be all right.

He hoped so. But there was Dandy Cabe to face—and Lanny and Tom. Winning Vaughan over was a big step, but there were other steps to be taken. He sighed and turned Lady. He would worry about those steps when they were ready to be taken.

CHAPTER FOUR

He was at Vaughan's house before seven the next morning. That meant getting up before daylight to make the ride here. Last night Paw had whined about who was going to do the plowing and how could it be done with only one horse. Ashel shut him up by saying, "You're lucky we're able to do any plowing at all. Hobe and Nobby got us into this. Let them work it out the best way they can." He had no sympathy for his brothers. Because of them, he had a month of bondage ahead of him, and it could be a rough month.

Vaughan came out of the house. He broke off a yawn as he saw Ashel and said, "You're here early enough." He sounded as though he regretted yesterday's decision. "You can back out now." His eyes were challenging.

Ashel said flatly, "We made a deal."

An angry flash appeared in Vaughan's eyes. "Yes," he said curtly. "I haven't got time this morning to lay out any work. Do whatever Mrs. Vaughan wants done."

He strode past Ashel toward one of the barns.

Ashel watched him until he disappeared, then looked at the house. Millie Vaughan was just coming out of the door, drying her hands on her apron. She read something in the blankness of Ashel's face and said, "Don't mind Milo. His bark is a lot worse than his bite. Have you eaten?"

"Yes, ma'am," he lied.

"You can put your horse in the barn. Give her some oats."

He thought he saw pity in her eyes, and a stiffness set his face. He did not want pity. He just wanted to work off a debt.

She followed him to the barn and asked, "Did you ever milk a cow?"

She was trying to be friendly, and he could not help but respond to it. "Yes, ma'am. We had a cow back in Missouri." He was suddenly horribly homesick—homesick for a damned cow.

"Milo fought me for months before he would consent to getting a milk cow. Now, he brags that fresh milk and butter were his idea."

Her laughter drew a smile from Ashel. She was a warm, giving woman, somewhere in her early forties, and Vaughan was a lucky man. Ashel knew her house would be clean and orderly. He wondered if there were any children. So far he saw no evidence of any.

"I still have to fight the men about milking her," she said. "They've sneaked off again this morning. You saw how Milo hurried away. Tonight they'll tell me they forgot again. If you can do it, it will help me."

"I'll be glad to," he said and meant it.

The Guernsey cow was in the corral, and he drove her into the barn. He fastened her head in the stanchion and poured out oats before her. She watched him with suspi-

40

cious eyes before she lowered her head and began eating. A milk cow was always distrustful with a stranger.

Millie handed him a bucket. He shook his head and set it down. He had to make friends with the cow before he started milking.

He stood beside her, keeping up a low, crooning talk. He stroked her until she did not flinch at his touch. When the petting did not interrupt her eating, he reached for the pail. There was no milking stool, and he squatted on his heels. He reached for her teats, and his hands were gentle. A cow hated rough handling.

Her teats were the right size for milking. Some cows had teats too small, and a man had to exert pressure to get milk from them. Others were too large, making it hard to grip them. He kept up an even, gentle pull, and the milk splashed into the bucket. He never broke the low rhythm of his words, and the cow stood loose and relaxed as she ate. It took him ten minutes to milk and strip her out, and the bucket was almost full.

Millie looked wide-eyed at it. "You're a magician. None of the other men ever get over half that much."

He set the bucket on a shelf and released the cow. He drove her out of the barn, slapping her on the hip as she left. "She's a good cow," he said. "Maybe they holler and swear at her. Men, hating to milk, would do that."

"They do."

"That scares a cow. A scared cow holds her milk up."

She reached for the bucket, and his hand was ahead of hers. "I'll carry it in. When it cools, I'll churn."

"That's another chore everybody ducks." She hesitated, then said, "I don't know your name."

"Ashel. Ashel Backus."

"That was an honest thing you did yesterday afternoon, Ashel. It won't turn out as bad as you think it will."

He remembered the rage on Tom's and Lanny's faces; he remembered Dandy Cabe. He still had to hear from them. He said, "Yes, ma'am," and his face was blank.

She sighed as she moved on ahead of him. He was a hard one to reach. For a moment during the milking, there had been understanding between them. It was a fragile thing, and if it came back into existence it would have to be nursed very carefully. She saw a combination of pride, hurt, and suspicion in him. When a man blended those things and pulled it around him, it made a tough armor to penetrate.

He set the bucket of milk in the kitchen and came out again, ignoring the rumbling of his stomach. It had been a long time since he had drunk a glass of fresh milk.

He said, "Stovewood is getting low," and walked to the woodpile.

Four armloads filled the box beside the stove. He stopped on the last trip and looked about the kitchen. This was a big room and used only for a kitchen. With nothing piled up in its corners, extending out so that a person stumbled over it. With a place for everything and everything clean. He shook his head at the luxury.

He went back to the woodpile and chopped and split wood the rest of the morning. He had it piled up like a small mountain when he finally put the ax aside. It needed sharpening before he cut more wood. A man was foolish to use his muscles instead of a keen edge.

He moved back to the kitchen, and Milo Vaughan must

have returned without him seeing him, for he heard his voice coming from inside the house. "What about the new man, Millie?" Vaughan asked.

"Milo, I wish you'd talk to him."

"Not working out, eh? I was afraid of that."

Ashel's face froze. He felt the angry hurt pumping through him. What else did they expect?

"Not working out," she cried. "Go look at that woodpile. He cut more wood this morning than your lazy bunch would cut in a week. I can't make him stop. He can't keep on working like that."

"Say now," Vaughan said. "Isn't that fine. It makes a man feel pretty good to put out trust and have it handed back with something added."

The tension eased in Ashel. Maybe she was right. Maybe it was going to work out. He retreated some twenty yards, and when he came forward again he was whistling. Not a loud, joyous whistling, but enough to let them know he was coming.

Vaughan came to the door and said, "Come in here."

Ashel stepped into the kitchen. It was filled with the aroma of freshly baked bread. The saliva started in his mouth and there was exquisite torture in his stomach.

"Sit down, Ashel," Millie said. She put a huge slab of warm bread before him and poured a glass of milk.

Vaughan buttered a piece of bread. "I'd rather eat fresh bread than cake." He frowned as Ashel sparingly used the butter. "Man, you don't know how to butter a piece of bread. Give me that." He took the slice from Ashel, spread butter a quarter-inch thick, and handed it back. He grinned as Ashel took the first bite. "That's something, isn't it?"

Ashel met the grin. It was something. He ate it slowly, savoring it to the last crumb. He shook his head at her offer of another slice. He wanted it. Good God, how he wanted it. "No, ma'am," he said. "That's enough." He was grateful she did not press him.

"Milo," she said. "We're almost out of butter. If I have to churn, I won't get through today."

Vaughan groaned. "When I'm eating it, I think it's worth it. When I'm on that churn, I wonder about the worth."

Ashel remembered how monotonous a job churning was. A person sat for a long time, working the handle of the plunger up and down. It seemed forever before the butter started coming.

He said, "I used to hate that job. Back in Missouri, I figured out a way to beat it. I'll need a small keg and a saw."

Vaughan's eyes were interested. "I've got a whisky keg. Will that do?"

"That will do fine."

He went with Vaughan to get the keg and saw.

"You bring it back here," Millie called after them. "I want to see what you're doing."

He carried the keg from the barn to the kitchen steps. He smelled at the hole in the top of the keg. The whisky odor still lingered.

"If you're going to make butter in that, won't it make it taste like whisky?" Millie asked.

Vaughan laughed. "Would that be bad?"

Ashel grinned at the look on her face. "No, ma'am. It won't taste."

He sawed a small door in the side of the keg and kept the piece, affixing small straps of leather to it to act as hinges.

He laid the piece back over the hole and tacked the hinges into place. He cut another strap of leather and tacked it over the door to keep it from flying open. As he worked he said, "The first time I tried this, I forgot I had to have a way to get the butter out. I had to cut a door in the keg after the butter was made. It tasted of sawdust."

He rinsed out the keg, set it on its end, and poured in the cream from several milkings. Millie's face was dubious as she watched.

He corked the keg and hoisted it to his shoulder. That much cream amounted to some weight. "Now, I need a horse," he told Vaughan. Lady would not do. She was too old and tired. He needed one with a little life. He doubted Vaughan kept any other kind around.

Vaughan nodded. "I think I know what you're going to do. Blackie is out in the barn. He won't like carrying that keg."

"Most of them don't," Ashel said.

He set the keg down, while he saddled. Blackie's eyes rolled until the muddy whites showed. He distrusted strangers, too. Ashel smoothed out the saddle blanket, running his hands over it until the last wrinkle was gone.

Vaughan's expression showed approval. He liked a man who was considerate of a horse.

Ashel kept up a low stream of words, but he was not going to talk Blackie out of anything. He cinched up the saddle, tested it, then thumped Blackie in the barrel to make him exhale the breath he was holding. He drew the cinch up another notch.

Vaughan nodded as though confirming something to himself. This man had been around horses enough to know what to expect from them.

Ashel lashed the keg behind the saddle, the door-side up. He led Blackie out of the barn.

Vaughan said, "He hasn't been ridden for a couple of weeks. He'll pitch until he gets the cussedness out. Do you want me to take him?"

Ashel felt a small start of resentment. All the cattlemen thought a homesteader was helpless when he got his feet off the ground. "I can handle it."

He swung into the saddle and said, "Let him go."

Vaughan let go and stepped aside.

Blackie put his head down and climbed for height. He landed on a stiffened foreleg, and the resultant shock snapped Ashel's head forward, then back. He opened his mouth and yelled for the sheer joy of it. It had been a long time since he knew good horseflesh under him.

A half-dozen jumps convinced Blackie this was not the answer to dislodging rider or keg. He came down the last time and lit out of the corral gate at a hard run. Ashel let him go until the animal was willing to stop of his own choice. He whirled him and galloped him back. He kept him moving hard for better than twenty minutes, and Blackie was sweated and blowing, when Ashel finally let him stop.

He swung down and handed the reins to Vaughan. He unlashed the keg and set it on the ground. "I'll dry him off," he said.

He led the horse into the barn and rubbed him dry with a gunny bag he found. He poured out oats for him, and Blackie's eyes still rolled. It was going to take more than a few oats to make up to Blackie for the indignities he had just been through.

By the time Ashel got back to the kitchen Vaughan was finishing spooning butter out of the keg. "It works," he said, and he sounded as tickled as a keg. "That chore is over."

Millie molded the butter into large, golden mounds. She looked at Ashel, and her eyes were shining.

Ashel smiled with them. It was a shared moment of accomplishment, rich and rewarding. "It works pretty good," he said and turned to leave.

"Where are you going?" Vaughan demanded.

"I noticed the box stalls could stand some cleaning."

"Let it go. You've earned it."

Ashel shook his head and continued on his way. He could not pay off the forty dollars by sitting around.

He was finished by six o'clock. That pile of manure outside the barn door was going to have to be carted away. Perhaps in the morning he could get a wagon and team and move it.

He heard voices as he reached the door and halted. He recognized both of them. He should; he heard them only yesterday morning.

"We should've stayed out later," Lanny grumbled. "You know it's the day Millie churns."

"And make her madder than ever," Tom said. "Besides, I got nothing to duck. It's your time."

"It is like hell," Lanny exploded. "I remember I did it last time."

"Neither of you has to worry," Milo Vaughan said. "It's all done."

"Ah." Lanny's voice sounded troubled. "Did Millie

do it again?"

"Nope."

"You didn't do it?" Lanny was incredulous.

"I hired a new man this morning. He figured out a way to beat that chore." Vaughan told them about the keg. "Blackie's running sloshes the cream around until it turns to butter."

"That's pretty damn smart," Tom said. "I guess none of us will argue about doing it any more. Where is this man?"

"Ashel," Vaughan called.

Ashel stepped out of the barn. The knot was back in his stomach.

Lanny stared at him, then his face darkened. "It's him," he yelled. "The one who took our guns. It's that damned Honyocker we told you about."

He started forward, and Vaughan said, "Lanny." The note in his voice stopped Lanny short. "He's trying to pay off a debt. You'd give a man a chance, wouldn't you?"

"Not him," Lanny said fiercely.

Tom looked at Ashel with speculative eyes. "His crazy brothers would probably have shot us. He kept them from doing it. Besides, that butter stunt ought to be worth something to us. We can go along, Lanny, and see how it turns out."

The hard knot dissolved into looseness. Millie Vaughan said it would work out all right. So far she was right. They were not offering him friendship, but the sharp edge of their hostility was blunted. There was still Dandy Cabe to face. Dandy was different from any of them.

CHAPTER FIVE

Dandy Cabe said, "I gave Ackerman fifty dollars to get out of the country on."

Pete shook his head. "You didn't have to give him anything."

"It was cheap at that price. He signed his land over to me." The fifty dollars was not all the inducement Ackerman had. He had a burned barn and a dead milk cow. The weather, combined with other misfortunes, whipped him. He was glad enough to take the money, as small as it was. His signing over the deed made everything legal. Nothing could kick back on Cabe now.

Ackerman's land made the third quarter section Cabe had picked up this spring. A little intimidation, a little terror, plus the natural discouragement of the country, made these Honyockers eager enough to run. He said, "They didn't belong here in the first place. Plowing up grass land."

Pete bobbed his head in agreement. He asked, "Dandy, why are you so anxious to own land all of a sudden? You must be putting every cent you got into it."

Cabe was. Plus a good night's winning at the poker table. He said, "Every man wants to own land. I'm going to be the equal of Milo one of these days." His eyes were bleak as he stared off into space. Milo and the others got here when a man could grab off immense chunks of land. There was no such opportunity now. Sometimes his pace of acquiring land was maddeningly slow, but he never lost his patience. He picked out a homesteader at a time and worked on him until the Honyocker was ready to leave. A quarter of a section here and a quarter there, and it mounted up. Pete and Lanny hated the homesteaders as much as he did, and they thought Milo was too soft with them. They were willing to help him, and they enjoyed terrorizing the Honyockers. It gave answer to a need in their wild, reckless natures. When he was ready, he would build a good crew around them.

Pete said, "If Milo finds out, he'll fire us all."

Cabe shook his head. "He won't find out until I'm ready to quit. Then, well leave him high and dry."

"If the Honyockers work together, they can stop us," Pete said.

Cabe's eyes danced with silent laughter. "Then the cattlemen will band to meet them. But it won't happen. None of them have the guts of a scared rabbit." He hoped it would come to open warfare. The homesteaders would be driven out in droves, and a vast amount of land would be up for grabs. If it happened, he would be in the front ranks, grabbing with both hands. But he would not count on it happening. The homesteaders might grumble about what was happening to a neighbor, but they could point their finger at no one. It was impossible to identify men on a quick, nighttime raid. The homesteaders accused and jumped all the cattlemen or no one. It was a perfect setup.

Pete was worrying an idea around in his head. He said, "You never were hungry for land before. Even last year, you didn't seem—" His eyes narrowed and he said, "Say, you started talking about it right after Miss Jenny went back to school, last fall. She comes back right away for good. Is she your reason?"

Cabe could not keep the color from his face. Jenobia Vaughan was never out of his thoughts these past months. She liked him. He knew that. If he could go to Milo Vaughan and say, "Look. I've got land. I can support your daughter," Vaughan would not refuse him. He would have no reason to refuse him.

Pete saw Cabe's expression and laughed. "So, that's it. That's what's driving you. Aren't you kinda old for her, Dandy?"

Cabe's face turned murderous. He reached over and fastened both hands in Pete's shirt front. "Don't say that." His voice shook with his fury. He was thirty-five, and Jenobia was nineteen. He was not too old for her. "Don't ever say that again."

The look in Cabe's eyes frightened Pete. "Hell, Dandy," he protested. "I was just joking you. I didn't mean anything."

Cabe let go of him, the momentary flash of anger gone. Pete might think some things, but he would never mention them again. He was smart enough for that. As for other wagging tongues, he would take care of them as he came up against them. He squinted at the setting sun. "It's getting late. We'd better move. Millie will be sore, if we're late for supper again."

Vaughan said, "You'd better come along and get cleaned up. Millie wants to have as early a supper as she can. Dandy and Pete should be along in a few minutes."

Ashel said, "I'd better be getting home." He could not avoid seeing Cabe again, but one more night would help.

Vaughan shook his head. "You're not in that big a hurry.

Millie would raise hell if you left." He started to say something else, then turned his head. Ashel heard it, too, the sound of hoofs.

"That will be Dandy and Pete," Vaughan said.

The hollow in Ashel's stomach was making him sick. It was too late to run. Maybe Cabe would accept him as Tom and Lanny had. Maybe— He let it go. He was only kidding himself.

Cabe and Pete rode up to the four men. Even with dust on his boots and his shirt sweat-stained after a day's work, Cabe still looked the dandy. He swung down with a flourish. He did everything that way. Even standing still, there was the suggestion of a swagger about him.

He said, "Milo, the north fork is drying up pretty fast."

Vaughan looked worried. "How much longer will it last, Dandy?"

"Maybe a couple of weeks. We'll have to move that bunch of cows then."

Ashel was trying to stand behind Lanny, and Cabe caught his first glimpse of him. His mouth momentarily loosened. Then it tightened into a cruel line. "Well, well. What have we got here?"

Vaughan missed the gleam in Cabe's eyes. "A new man, Dandy. He's working off a debt."

Cabe grinned at Pete. "Can you imagine that, Pete? The Honyocker rode out here to pay off some debts." He stripped the gloves from his hands. "I guess now's the time to start collecting."

Vaughan caught his intent. "Dandy," he said sharply. "Let him alone."

Cabe fixed him with hard eyes. "Milo, this is a personal

matter. You going to interfere with it?"

Ashel saw the spot in which Vaughan was caught. Cabe was forcing Vaughan to pick a side. He said, "Let it be, Mr. Vaughan. I guess it had to come sometime."

He balled his hands and crouched. "All right, Cabe."

Cabe grinned wickedly as he moved forward. The men spread about them, forming a rough ring. "Bust him, Dandy," Lanny said savagely. The edge was back on Lanny's hostility.

"Don't kill him, Dandy," Pete whooped. "Just mess him up enough so that he wishes he was dead."

Cabe came at Ashel in a rush. He threw his right hand in an awkward but powerful blow. Ashel jerked his head aside, and the knuckles grazed his cheek. He felt the stinging, and the hollow in his stomach was filling—filling with rage. He sank his fist in Cabe's stomach, and the force of his swing, plus Cabe's momentum, made it a good blow. It rocked Cabe back a step, and his breath left him in a loud *oof.* He rubbed his belly, and a ferocious glitter was in his eyes.

"You're running up the bill," he said and came again.

Ashel met the rush with one of his own. He was up against a heavier, more powerful man. It would take telling blows to drain some of that power away.

He hit Cabe in the stomach again, pulling a grunt from him. He bounced his knuckles off Cabe's cheekbone, and Cabe roared in pure anger. He threw his punches with rapid desperation, and Cabe still came. Something that felt like a club landed on the side of his jaw. His head flew backwards, jerking him off his feet. He landed heavily, the dust puffing up around him. His eyes would not focus, and his world swung and dipped.

He could hear Pete's and Lanny's laughter, and the sound filled him with murderous hatred. He raised his fingers to his mouth, and when he drew them away there was blood on them.

"Get up," Cabe said. "You haven't collected it all."

Ashel tried to focus on him, but Cabe would not stand still. He weaved from side to side, he swelled in size, then diminished. One thing remained fixed—his mocking grin. It seemed almost separate from him, hanging in the air, the infuriating twist of it making Ashel's soul sick with rage. It pulled him to his feet and drove him forward.

He tried to hit that grin with both fists to blot it out. His right hand hit something solid, and it felt good. Someone far away grunted. Then he was on his back again, and the buzzing in his head changed to a persistent drum. The grin still hung in the air before him.

"You had enough?" The words seemed to come from far behind the grin.

He pushed to his feet much more slowly. It demanded exertion that pulled sobs from him. He made it and shuffled forward. He had to hit that grin just one more time.

He swung, and his fist seemed to go right through it. He could not make the damned thing disappear, and his sobbing was louder. He was on his back again, and he did not know how he got there, for he felt nothing. The drumming in his head was worse. He sat up and put his hands to his head to ease that awful drumming. When he took his hands away, both of them felt sticky. He looked curiously at the red smear on them without realizing what it was.

"You had enough?"

That was Cabe's voice, and it sounded a little wild. Now, why would that be? He thought about it, and his mind was too weary to hold onto anything.

His arms insisted upon buckling as he used them to pry himself up off the ground, and he had to will strength into them.

"My God," someone's awed voice said. "He's getting up again."

He had his direction. He could still see Cabe's grin, and he plodded toward it. He swung once, then again before he was back in the dust.

He lay there shaking his head, trying to escape the herd of horses that were stomping through it. He sat up, tasting the blood and the sour sickness in his mouth.

Cabe yelled, "Goddamn you. Stay down."

It sounded like a scream, and that was odd. What did Cabe have to scream about?

He had to crawl a few feet before his legs would support him. He raised himself with pain-wracked effort. He reeled as he stood and tried to pull up his head and hands. He had to hit Cabe just once more.

He saw only a blur of movement toward him and heard someone's whistling breath. He swung and connected, knowing by the dull jolt that ran up his arm. Then the ground was jerked from under his feet. He fell forward this time. Just spitting the dust out of his mouth was a colossal job.

"You get up again, and I'll kill you." Cabe's voice was broken and pitched high.

Ashel thought, he sounds like he's scared, and it was a ridiculous idea. What did Cabe have to be frightened of?

He crawled a longer distance this time, and when he got to his knees, he had to rest. He pulled to his feet, grunting like an animal. The grin was coming at him, and he swung a fist that seemed to have weights hanging from it. It landed right in the middle of that grin, and he had the hazy impression that red spurted from it.

He could be wrong, but he thought he fell rather than was knocked down. He felt no pain, only that over-powering weariness. It would be easier not to try to get up, but some thought he could not quite get hold of would not let him rest. He rolled over, clutching at the dust for purchase.

"Jesus," a faint voice said. "He's getting up."

He made it to his hands and knees and crawled like a wounded animal. He did not see Cabe's blood-smeared, twisted face, or the start of his rush. He vaguely heard Cabe yell, "I'll stomp your damned head off." He did not see Vaughan throw his body into Cabe, blocking his charge, or hear Vaughan say, "None of that, Dandy. Let him get up."

"Jesus," Lanny muttered again as he watched Ashel struggle to climb to his feet.

Tom shook his head. "I never saw anything like it," he muttered.

Pete stood silent, an awed look on his face.

Ashel got to his knees and fell back. He did not know tears were streaking his face, tears of rage at his impotent strength. He could not get up yet, but he could crawl, crawl until enough strength returned to get to his feet.

He was crawling, his head hanging, his arms buckling and threatening to dump him, when Millie Vaughan came around the corner of the barn.

Her eyes blazed as she took in the scene. Cabe stood on

widely braced legs, his chest heaving. He wiped the back of a hand across his lips, looked at the blood on it, and shook his head. He stared at Ashel, and there was an uneasy flickering in his eyes.

Millie said passionately, "Dandy Cabe, you ought to be ashamed of yourself."

Cabe kept his eyes on Ashel. If he heard her, he gave no indication.

She said, "You'll be sorry for this. Wait and see." She turned on Milo. "You! Why did you let it happen?"

Vaughan took a defensive, backward step. "Millie, it was just something that couldn't be stopped. They both told me to stay out of it."

She glared at him, then said to Tom, "Help me get him into the house."

Ashel fought their hands as they tried to lift him to his feet. "Ashel," Millie said. "You come along now. You hear me?"

The fight went out of him, and he would have fallen without their support. Tom put Ashel's arm over his shoulder, and Millie supported him from the other side. He tried to walk, and his feet left dragging furrows in the dust. They went around the corner of the barn, and Millie's voice drifted back. "Just a little farther, Ashel. Just a few more steps."

Cabe looked from face to face. He stared longest at Vaughan.

"I whipped him," he said. "I whipped him good."

Vaughan watched him with cold, speculative eyes. He still retained a picture of Ashel crawling toward Cabe.

"You didn't whip him, Dandy." He shook his head, the

gesture lending emphasis to his words. "You might've marked him up some. But you sure didn't whip him."

CHAPTER SIX

The touch of the wet cloth brought back full consciousness to Ashel. It was worse this way. Every bruise, every cut set up its individual clamor, and the mass voice of them was as much as he wanted to stand. He winced and jerked as the cloth moved over his cheek, and Millie made a distressed sound.

He tried to smile at her, and the pain took the smile and distorted it into a grimace. He couldn't see very well. One eye was completely closed, and the other was just a slit.

Tom stood back of Millie, judiciously watching her work. "I never seen anything like it," he kept saying. Admiration was in his voice. "He kept getting up and coming back for more."

Millie turned on him like an enraged whirlwind. "And all of you thought it was wonderful. None of you would step in and stop it."

Tom's face was pained. "Aw, Millie. We couldn't stop it. It was a personal matter."

"And that made it sacred. But not sacred enough to keep you from whooping and cheering while this happened. All of you are animals. Just animals."

Tom was a few feet from the door, and he bolted for it.

Millie's face was still indignant as she turned back to finish her work. She had most of the blood from Ashel's face, and the cuts had stopped bleeding. He looked terrible, simply terrible. The bruises were swelling and coloring. By tomorrow, he would look even worse.

In defense of Tom, Ashel said, "It wasn't his fault. He had nothing to do with it."

"It was all their fault," she snapped. "Just wait until I talk to Milo. And Dandy. Mr. Dandy Cabe will be sorry for this." The anger faded from her voice, and she asked, "Why, Ashel? Why did you go ahead? Dandy's bigger and stronger than you."

He thought vaguely about it, then said, "I guess I just couldn't help it."

Millie wrung out the cloth in the pan. The water was a deep pinkish color. "I'll never understand men. Never."

Milo Vaughan came into the room. He looked at Ashel and said heartily, "Boy, you're looking better." He talked to Ashel, but his eyes shifted uneasily to Millie and back. "Dandy didn't get off too easy. He'll remember this night for a long time." He looked at Millie and winced. He knew that rigid attitude too well.

Ashel thought, I'll remember it, too. Longer than Dandy. But Cabe might let him alone now. He hoped so. He fervently hoped so.

Vaughan said, "Millie, the boys are asking about supper. They're getting pretty hungry."

Millie's eyes looked wild for a moment, and Vaughan thought she was going to explode. He asked plaintively, "What did I say wrong now?"

She contained herself with visible effort. "Fix it yourself." She stalked toward an inner door. "Men," she said as she slammed it behind her.

Vaughan gave Ashel a rueful grin. "I've lived with her for twenty-two years, and I don't understand her yet."

Ashel guessed Millie had the same complaint in reverse. He got to his feet, and it cost effort. His ribs and chest were a great throbbing drum, but he could walk.

He started for the door, and Vaughan protested, "You're not going home tonight."

"Yes." The word came out harsh. He didn't intend it that way, but the pain put grit in his voice.

Vaughan caught the determination and let that point drop. "You can't leave before you've eaten. Millie's got it on the stove. All I have to do is—" His words faded away at Ashel's shaking head.

Ashel could not bear the thought of food. And to sit at the table with everyone putting covert glances on him— He could not bear that, either.

"Then take Blackie. You'll make it faster."

Blackie was a spirited horse. If he pitched tonight, Ashel thought, it'd kill me. He said, "I don't think I could take Blackie tonight, Mr. Vaughan."

As he went out the door he heard Vaughan's soft swearing. It had a helpless sound.

He passed Lanny and Pete on his way to the barn. If they say anything to me, he thought wildly, I'll— It was useless to finish the thought. No matter what they said, he couldn't do anything to them. He couldn't do anything to anybody.

They stared at him wooden-faced, then turned their heads. He moved past them to the barn and led Lady out of it. It was going to be rough mounting her. He sucked in his breath for the effort and scrambled onto her back. It stirred the dull aches into vivid life. His head hung on his chest, and his world was hazy for a moment. He lifted his head and started Lady at a slow walk. He passed Lanny and

Pete, and they did not look at him. He went by the house, and when he was fifty yards away from it, he heard Millie calling his name. Her voice had a frantic note, but he did not look around. If he listened to her entreaties, he would weaken. He would fall right off this horse.

It was almost dark, when he neared the Reynolds' place, and he hoped both of them were inside. He groaned as he saw Clell and Cassie in front of the house.

"Hold up, Ashel," Reynolds yelled.

He could keep on going and pretend he didn't hear the order, but that would be a gross affront to Reynolds. It would drive the wedge deeper and push Cassie farther away from him.

He sighed and hauled on the reins.

Reynolds came toward him, his face heavy with accusation. "I saw you go by early this morning. You spent the whole day out there. What kind of dealings take that long?"

For the first time he realized how battered Ashel's face was, and his expression changed. "Hah," he said. "You had trouble with them. I knew it'd happen. I guess Vaughan did it. Maybe you know now which side you belong on."

"It wasn't Vaughan. And I'm going back tomorrow." Reynolds might as well know it now. "I'm working for Vaughan."

Reynolds had trouble finding his tongue, then he roared, "Why, you goddamned idiot. After a beating like you took and you still don't know who your friends are. You stay away from here. You hear me. Stay away."

He turned and almost bumped into Cassie. "Come along, Cassie," he ordered, and strode toward the house.

Cassie moved a step nearer Ashel, and her eyes brimmed

61

with tears. "Your poor face," she whispered.

He said wryly, "I'll live."

With a woman's intuition, she said, "It was Dandy Cabe, wasn't it?"

"It was Cabe."

"You can't go back," she cried. "He'll do it again."

Ashel shook his head. No, Cabe would not do it again. If Cabe tried to lay hands on him, he would pick up a club, or anything that was handy. He wouldn't try to stand up to Cabe again with only his bare hands.

"Cassie," Reynolds roared from the porch. "Are you coming, or do I have to come after you."

"You'd better go," Ashel said gently. "Everything will be all right."

She didn't believe him. Nothing was going to be all right. She whirled before he could see the tears starting from her eyes and ran toward the house.

Ashel stared at the closed door a long time before he kicked Lady into motion. He thought fiercely, I'll see her. I'll see her, whenever I'm ready, and nobody will stop me. It was a brave thought, built around nothing, and he knew how hollow it was.

He was exhausted, when he reached home. He slid off Lady and had to lean against her for a moment. Elodia ran out of the house, and he said, "Put her in the shed and feed her for me."

She said cheerfully, "Sure, Ashel," and took the reins.

He heard her talking to the horse as she led it inside the shed. He was glad the darkness hid his battered face. If she did not scream, she would at least cry.

He dreaded stepping into the light. They would throw a

hundred questions at him, questions he didn't feel like answering.

His mother saw him first and her face went white. "There's been trouble," she said tragically. "All day long, I been feeling it, and now it's happened." She started to cry, putting her face down into her apron.

"There hasn't been any trouble, Maw," he said as gently as he could. He was battered and sore, both in body and spirit. Her crying wasn't helping him at all.

Hobe had mean satisfaction on his face. "You tried to get smart with them like you did with us. They just about stomped your head off, didn't they?"

Ashel stared at him with his one good eye. The hot spark in it grew bigger and bigger. "Shut up, Hobe." He said it calmly enough, but it carried something, for Hobe looked at the floor. He muttered something to Nobby that Ashel didn't catch. Nobby looked at the wall. He hadn't missed that hot spark.

Paw said mournfully, "You had trouble with Vaughan. He wouldn't accept your offer to work for him. He'll be coming after us now."

"I didn't have trouble with Vaughan," Ashel said sharply. "And I'm going back tomorrow to work for him. Everything's all right." He picked up his pallet from the corner. He had to get away from them.

Paw said, "Then you're taking Lady again tomorrow."

"Yes." The word was curt.

"I don't know how we're going to get the plowing done," Paw wailed, "with just one horse."

Ashel left the house. His mother was still crying. Not a damned one of them asked how bad he was hurt.

"Ashel," Paw cried. "You come back here. I'm not through talking to you."

Ashel never checked his stride. He walked beyond the reach of the light and spread his pallet on the ground. All he wanted to do was to lie down and die until morning.

He didn't know anyone was near until a small hand timidly touched him. "Ashel," an equally timid voice said.

He turned his head toward his sister. "Yes, kid?"

"Are you hurt bad? Hobe and Nobby were laughing about it."

"I'm not hurt bad."

"I hate them," she said passionately.

He reached out and touched her face. It felt wet. Elodia was crying, and it made him feel like crying. "Don't pay any attention to them. They don't know any better."

She threw her arms around his neck and kissed him. Her kiss hurt his bruised cheek. He did not wince.

He said, "You get to bed, Elodia. It's late."

He lay awake a long time after she left. He wished sleep would come and blanket some of this aching.

CHAPTER SEVEN

Ashel cautiously attacked the manure pile. The first couple of swings with the fork were rough, making his muscles scream with the effort. But after he got into the rhythm of it, it wasn't so bad. In fact, he thought he might even work out the soreness quicker this way than by letting nature take its course.

He had the wagon half full, when Vaughan came around the corner of the barn. "What the hell are you doing?"

Vaughan yelled.

"Loading manure." Ashel never broke the rhythm of his swing.

"Dammit. I can see." Vaughan sounded angry. "I couldn't believe it when Millie told me what you were doing. I didn't even expect you today."

Ashel straightened and leaned his fork against the wagon. "I'm sorry I was late this morning." He had overslept a couple of hours, and then the stiffness slowed his movements.

"Oh, hell," Vaughan said helplessly.

Ashel reached for the fork, and Vaughan said, "Put it down."

Ashel shook his head. "It helps work the soreness out." He had made a deal with Vaughan. He couldn't pay his end by sitting around.

Vaughan said, "Oh, hell," again. He went into the barn and came back with another fork. "Let's get the damned job done then."

They worked in silence for fifteen minutes, and the manure pile melted into nothingness. When Vaughan straightened, his face was streaming. "I know better than to try to keep up with you young roosters," he grumbled.

He grinned at Ashel. "Have you seen your face this morning?"

It was a friendly question, carrying no malice. Ashel tried to return the grin. "I caught a glimpse of it. I couldn't bear to look any more." He was a sight. His good eye was open a little wider, and he could see light through the other one. He had enough color in his face to paint a couple of rainbows.

"Ashel." Vaughan stopped. He seemed to be searching for the right words. "I talked to Dandy. There won't be any more trouble."

"I'm glad." It wasn't hard for Ashel to mean that.

Vaughan let out a relieved sigh. He wouldn't have blamed Ashel for carrying a grudge. "I'm thirsty," he said. "Let's go to the house for a drink."

"I noticed a couple of the corral posts were sagging, Mr. Vaughan. If I tamp some rock in around them—"

"Dammit," Vaughan said. "Don't you ever listen to me?"

Ashel said, "Maybe I am thirsty." He liked this man. He hoped Vaughan liked him, too.

When they entered the kitchen, Millie's eyes were distressed as she looked at Ashel's face. She said coldly, "Milo, you know better than to let him be working like he was."

Vaughan said plaintively, "I made him quit, didn't I?" He gave Ashel a covert wink.

Ashel said, "He did, Mrs. Vaughan." He suspected Vaughan caught a lot of jawing last night. A man was helpless against it.

"I'm Milo," Vaughan said. "And she's Millie. It makes us uncomfortable to be called anything else."

"Yes, sir." Ashel felt a wet looseness behind his eyes. He didn't have to keep up his defenses around these people. The smell of warm gingerbread filled the kitchen, and his belly hurt, reminding him he had not eaten last night, or this morning.

Vaughan asked, "Millie, isn't that gingerbread ready to cut?"

"It is," she said, and moved to the oven. She cut Ashel a

slab she had to use both hands to lift. She remembered the look in his eyes as he finished the slice of bread yesterday.

Vaughan set milk and butter on the table. "I taught you how to spread butter yesterday."

He watched Ashel and said, "That's a little better." He took his first bite, and said, "Ah."

It was effort to keep from wolfing it down. Ashel could not remember when he had eaten anything that tasted so good. He couldn't empty his glass. Every time he took a drink Millie refilled it.

She offered him another piece, and he said honestly, "I couldn't." His belly was filled, and he felt loose and relaxed.

Vaughan stood and stretched. "I got to be getting back."

Ashel started to push to his feet, and Vaughan said, "Millie, didn't you tell me you had some things for him to do today?"

Ashel caught the exchange of glances between them. She thought quickly, for she said with only a moment's hesitation, "I have."

Vaughan looked back from the door. "You'd better keep the boss pleased."

Ashel's chin set in a stubborn jut. He knew what they were trying to do; they were trying to protect him. "I feel all right." He didn't want them babying him.

"Oh, hell," Vaughan said helplessly, and shut the door.

Ashel started to follow him, and Millie touched his arm. "If you're handy with tools, I do need you. The window is stuck in one of the bedrooms. Milo's been promising to fix it for two months, but—" She shrugged, and the gesture expressed the infinite patience a woman must have.

His eyes were suspicious, but he followed her into the room. It was a kind of frilly room, and he was surprised Milo would sleep in it.

The window was stuck all right. All his tugging couldn't budge it. He turned to Millie. "I can fix it if you have a plane."

"I think there's one in the toolshed."

He found the necessary tools in the shed. He came back with a hammer, a screwdriver, and the plane. It was nice to have the tools you needed when something needed fixing.

He pried off the trim and the stops, detached the sash cords and lifted the window from its casing. An eighth of an inch planed from each side ought to free the window.

He picked it up to carry outside, and as he turned, saw the picture on the dresser. It was the picture of a girl, somewhere around twenty he thought. He stood transfixed, struck by the beauty of her. Most people looked stiff and strained in a picture, but she didn't. She was laughing, and the infectious quality of it made him want to laugh in return. He had seen lots of pictures of actresses in the rotogravure sections, and he had thought them pretty. None of them could touch this girl.

Pride was in Millie's voice. "That's Jenobia. Our daughter."

Ashel realized he was staring and jerked his eyes from the picture. He could feel heat in his face and hoped it didn't show. He said lamely, "I hadn't seen her around." He said Jenobia in his mind. It had a pretty ring.

"She's away to school. This is her last year. She'll be coming home in a month."

He said, "I'll bet you've missed her." A month, he

thought with a queer kind of loss. He wouldn't be here.

"Yes," Millie said simply. "This is Jenny's room. That's why I want everything in it fixed."

He carried the window outside and planed it. He took longer than he should have, but he wanted it right. He kept seeing the picture, and he thought, you're acting pretty silly. A man doesn't feel this way over a picture. But there was a kind of tremble in his hands as he worked.

He took the window back and installed it. He could raise it with a finger.

Millie tried it several times. She looked at Ashel with shining eyes. "That's wonderful."

He smiled at the praise. He had a natural handiness with tools. He never got to use good ones very often. He hoped something else in this room needed fixing.

He asked, "What's next?"

"Could you fix a broken step on the front porch?"

He felt just a small disappointment. You're a damned fool, he told himself. He glanced at the picture as he left the room. She was looking directly at him and laughing. Not at me, he thought fiercely. She wouldn't do that.

He sawed a new tread and replaced the broken one. Some of the porch boards were beginning to rot, and he said, "I can fix that, too." He thought she was going to hug him.

"You're a treasure, Ashel. I keep after Milo, and he puts me off."

"He don't mean to put you off," Ashel said earnestly. "He just has bigger things on his mind."

"You stick together, don't you?" But she was smiling.

Ashel grinned. "I guess we do."

He spent the rest of the day repairing the porch. He couldn't get over the luxury of working with good tools and new material. He wished it could be that way at home. With the materials he had there, the fixing looked as bad as before he started.

He cut and fitted a board to the porch and before he started nailing it into place he heard the men ride in. He did not raise his head. But his heart was going faster. Dandy Cabe would be with them. Ashel wanted no further quarrel with him, but if Cabe persisted in pushing it, Ashel intended to use the hammer he held.

He heard the kitchen door slam and guessed Vaughan had entered the house. Millie's voice carried to him. "Go look at that window you promised to fix for me. And look at the front porch. If we can keep Ashel around here long enough, this place might look fit for humans to live in."

"He's making it hard for me to live here," Vaughan grumbled, but there was humor in his voice.

Cabe came around the house, leading his horse. He moved silently for Ashel did not hear him until he spoke.

"Get up from there, Honyocker. And put my horse away."

Ashel slowly straightened. The hammer swung in his hand. The bruises on Cabe's face gave him a deep satisfaction. The fight wasn't as one-sided as he thought it.

Cabe led a beautiful buckskin mare. Her tail and mane were jet black. She kept pushing at him, nuzzling his shoulder. She acted as though she liked him.

Ashel's chin set. This was only the first of a series of orders designed to humiliate him. And if he gave in to it, the others would pinch harder. He was working for Milo

70

Vaughan, not Dandy Cabe.

Before he could open his mouth to say so, Vaughan said from the front door, "Dandy, you in the habit of having someone put your horse away?"

Cabe threw him a startled glance.

"Then don't get started on it. It's a bad habit to break."

Color was high in Cabe's face, most of it from anger.

Vaughan said, "He's working for Millie. If you want him to do something, go through her."

Cabe searched for words, and Vaughan said calmly, "I'd just let it drop right here, Dandy."

Cabe turned and stalked away. The mare was still nuzzling him as he went around the corner.

Ashel breathed faster than he liked, and he was afraid Vaughan would take it for fear. "I wasn't going to put his horse away." He couldn't help the defiance in his voice.

"I didn't expect you to." Vaughan looked at the porch floor. "It's a nice job." He turned, then came back as though the thought just occurred to him. "Millie's expecting you to stay for supper."

Ashel shook his head. "Not tonight."

Exasperation built in Vaughan's face. "Dammit, Ashel. You can't be making that long ride twice a day. It'd be easier if you bunked and ate here."

It was sensible, and Ashel knew it. He continued to shake his head.

"Then take Blackie. He'll get you back here earlier in the morning." Vaughan grinned. "That way, I'll get more work out of you."

Ashel thought of how the family needed Lady for the plowing. He thought of that long, plodding ride on Lady and weakened. "I might do that," he said, not looking at Vaughan.

"Sure." Vaughan was already moving away. "Use the brown saddle that's hanging near his stall."

Ashel nailed the board in place, hammering hard to cover his feeling. Vaughan was an understanding man. He saw another's needs and made it easy for that person to accept help. Clell Reynolds is wrong about Vaughan, Ashel thought. I don't know about the other cattlemen, but Clell's wrong about him.

He put away the tools and walked toward the barn. He saddled Blackie without too much trouble. A few more times, and he and Blackie would get along well together.

He untied Lady's reins and led the two horses outside. Cabe and Pete stood just beyond the door.

Cabe said, "Well, well. What have we here? A little horse thieving?"

Holding Lady's reins, Ashel started to climb into the saddle. His leg was swinging over the cantle, when Cabe shied his hat under Blackie's belly.

Blackie needed little provoking. Ashel felt the horse's muscles bunch and dropped Lady's reins. He jammed his foot into the stirrup.

Blackie squalled and pitched. He did as thorough a job as he did yesterday morning. Ashel found that the bruises were not dead, only dormant. They came to life under the jolting. He felt like yelling again, not from exuberance, but from the hurting.

He grimly rode Blackie to a finish, and as the fight flowed out of the animal, he took a tight rein on him, not wanting him to break into a run. Blackie danced around in a circle, made an unconvincing effort at a last pitch, and stopped, breathing hard. Ashel breathed just as hard, but his head was carried high. No one would know that the pain in his ribs was clawing at him.

Vaughan was grinning, and Cabe and Pete stared at Ashel in slack-jawed wonder. Cabe's hat lay in the dust, thoroughly trampled. From its appearance, it looked as though Blackie did all his pitching from one tiny spot.

Vaughan said, "You didn't bargain for that surprise, did you, Dandy? I saw him ride yesterday morning."

The wonder was still in Pete's voice. "Dandy, he forked Blackie as well as you could."

Cabe threw him a murderous glance. He moved to his hat and started to pick it up. He swore at its battered appearance and left it lying there.

Vaughan winked at Ashel as he handed him Lady's reins.

Ashel nodded and prodded a subdued Blackie forward. He felt pretty good in spite of the hurt. He'd wrung praise out of Pete, and he'd given Cabe a shock. He couldn't want a much better evening.

He passed Reynolds' house, and Reynolds and Cassie were in the yard. Neither of them said a word as he rode by. Reynolds' face said it all. Ashel rode an M swinging V horse. That told everything as far as Reynolds was concerned.

Paw and Hobe and Nobby were outside, when Ashel arrived. Paw looked at the brand on Blackie, and his eyes went wild. "Good Lord," he cried. "He's stolen one of Milo Vaughan's horses."

Ashel controlled his irritation. "Milo lent him to me. You can have Lady for the plowing."

He swung down and started to strip the saddle from Blackie.

Hobe moved closer, his eyes glowing. "Leave it on," he ordered. "I was planning on going into town tonight. I'll take him."

"You'll keep your damned hands off him," Ashel said savagely. He would have to bring his pallet and sleep before the shed tonight.

The three were looking at Blackie with hunger in their eyes. Ashel couldn't blame them. It had been a long time since this good a piece of horseflesh had been on the place.

Paw said wistfully, "The plowing would go a lot faster, if we could use him."

Ashel almost grinned at the picture of Blackie harnessed before the plow. With his first plunge, that rotten, old harness would fly to pieces.

Ashel removed the saddle and led Blackie toward the shed. He said over his shoulder, "None of you touch him. I mean that."

Hobe's swearing carried to him clear inside the shed.

CHAPTER EIGHT

At the end of the first week Ashel gave in to Millie's and Vaughan's insistence and moved into the bunkhouse. It would save that twice daily long ride, and there was another reason, even stronger. Last night, Hobe had slipped by him and had Blackie saddled before Ashel was fully awake. Give Hobe a couple more minutes and he would have been off. What he would do then was anybody's guess. The least he would do would be to run Blackie into the ground. At worst, he would try to sell Blackie, or gamble him away. He had retreated before Ashel's flaming anger, saying sullenly, "Just you wait. Just wait."

That decided Ashel upon moving. Vaughan had lent Blackie to him, and no one else was going to touch him.

Maw cried all the time he packed his meager belongings. Paw kept saying, "I don't know how we're going to get along without you around."

"Good Lord," Ashel said finally. "I'll be back in three weeks."

He picked up the gunny bag that held his belongings and walked to the door. "Paw, it's getting late for planting. You'd better get that plowing done."

Paw mumbled something Ashel didn't catch. His manner was evasive as it was every time Ashel tried to talk about the plowing. Ashel thought, I'll bet they haven't done anything this whole damned week.

He pointed his finger at his father. "Paw, I mean it."

Paw looked abused. "Don't we always get it done?"

Yes, Ashel thought grimly. When I'm around to do it. He felt a sudden, helpless rage at his father and brothers. He left the house before the rage fashioned hot, tearing words.

Elodia waited for him outside, and she walked with him to the shed. He suspected there were tears behind the white stillness of her face. She grabbed his hand and said passionately, "Ashel, I'm going to miss you."

"Three weeks, kid." He snapped his thumb and forefinger. "It'll be gone like that." He raised her chin and gently touched each eyelid with a forefinger. "You help Maw all you can."

"I will," she promised. "I'll come when she calls me and

75

not hide out any more."

"That's good." He tousled her hair and mounted Blackie. He looked back after fifty yards. She stood rooted, watching him.

Kids have it tough, he thought. Who doesn't, he thought angrily. Who in the hell doesn't?

Cabe and Pete were in the bunkhouse when Ashel moved in. Cabe watched him pull his few possessions out of the gunny bag and said, "It looks like the ragpickers have moved in, Pete."

Ashel whirled, his face flaming. Before he could speak, Tom came through the door. He said, "I heard that, Dandy. I remember when I first went to work for Milo. My ass was almost bare, and my toes could nibble grass. But a little time and work changed that."

Cabe glared at him. "You've got a big mouth. Someday it's going to get you hurt."

Tom said cheerfully, "I'm a brittle old man, Dandy. You hit me, and they'll arrest you for murder."

Cabe stared at him with hot eyes, then stalked to the door. "Come on, Pete," he ordered, and Pete followed him.

Ashel's face was concerned. He felt he had three friends here. Millie and Vaughan—and now Tom. Cabe couldn't do anything to the first two, but he could make it rough on Tom. "I don't want you to have any trouble because of me."

Tom grinned. "An old man doesn't worry much about trouble. He's seen about all there is of it. I do my work, and Milo knows it. Dandy isn't going to push me around too much."

His face sobered. "I'm not going to tell you Dandy isn't

a hard man. He is. He can never forgive anyone who makes him look second best. You got a way of coming out on top against him, and he knows it. It's eating him pretty hard. He's going to hand you all the dirt he can. You'd better pray you stay lucky, or that Milo's around. But whatever happens keep your head. You can't beat him with your fists or a gun."

Ashel nodded. "Thanks, Tom. I intend to stay away from him all I can."

"That's smart." Tom stretched out on his bunk. "About twenty minutes to supper. Ain't that Millie the best cook you ever saw?"

Friday morning, Ashel was on the barn roof, replacing shingles the busy fingers of the wind had worried away. The supply of new shingles was getting low. He must remember to tell Milo they needed to split some more.

He lifted his head as he heard Vaughan and Cabe talking below him. He wasn't eavesdropping. His ladder leaned against the roof for anybody to see.

"Milo," Cabe said. "It's time to move that bunch around the north fork. It's gone dry except for a pothole or two. That water won't last more than a day or so."

Vaughan sighed. "We got a couple of weeks more grazing there than I thought. That's a little blessing, anyway. We'll get on it tomorrow."

"We can do it today. The men are all in."

"I'll saddle up and be right with you, Dandy."

"That's rough country around that creek, Milo. An extra hand would come in handy helping dig them out of the brush."

"You got somebody in mind, Dandy?"

"The Honyocker can ride. He's got enough sense to follow a cow, once she's pointed out of the brush, hasn't he?"

"Dandy, why can't you leave him alone? He's doing a job. A good one. Look at this place."

Cabe sounded injured. "Hell, I'm not picking on him. All I'm asking for is a little extra help."

Ashel heard the sound of Cabe's retreating footsteps. He leaned over the edge and said, "Mr. Vaughan."

Vaughan lifted his face. "Dammit. How many times do I have to tell you to quit calling me that?"

Ashel grinned. "Yes, sir." It was hard to get in the habit of saying "Milo." His face sobered. "I didn't mean to be listening."

"I saw the ladder. I figured you were up there."

Ashel climbed down. "Milo, I'd like to go. I can finish this tomorrow."

Vaughan's eyes were sharp. "Cows are Dandy's business, Ashel. He's probably got some thought in mind of showing you up."

"Yes," Ashel said recklessly. "But I can learn, can't I?" He also might earn a little respect. He didn't tell Vaughan how lonely the evenings grew in the bunkhouse. Tom talked to him, but the others ignored him.

Vaughan studied him, then said, "Come along, then." He would be with them. He would be there to thwart whatever Cabe had in mind.

It was good to be riding with them. Cabe had looked at him and said gruffly, "I'm glad you're here." His words gave Ashel's spirits a buoyant lift. Maybe he and Dandy could make it up between them.

The country lifted and grew rougher. Vaughan had little to say, but his eyes were alert. Ahead of them was a sharp upthrust of ground, densely covered with brush and stunted trees. Ashel saw the flitting forms of cattle beginning to move ahead of the riders. Excitement built in him. He was going to like this better than his job of handy man.

It took hard riding, some of it even dangerous, in turning back the cattle that persisted in trying to break through the thin line of horsemen. A man ducked and swayed in the saddle, or took a stinging slap in the face from some out-stretched limb. He had to be ready to move in the direction his horse moved, or a quick jump or spin could dump him.

More and more distance separated the men as they followed the twisting, turning cattle. Cows bawled, trying to locate their calves, showed stubborn fight for a moment, then moved on ahead of a pushing horseman. The steers were the spookiest of all, showing a tremendous burst of speed for a short distance. Ashel came back after turning a big yellow one back into line, and Cabe and Pete were there. He did not see Vaughan. In the milling confusion, they had become separated.

Cabe yelled, "Come on. A half dozen head broke back this way." He spurred away at breakneck speed. The buckskin mare was beautiful to watch, and she had the nimble feet of a goat.

Blackie could not keep up with either Cabe's or Pete's mounts and Ashel momentarily lost them, when he had to detour a sharp escarpment of rock. He rounded it, and the creek was before him, its bed dried and cracked. Farther on, he caught a glimpse of Cabe and Pete sitting motionless horses. An uneasy feeling touched him, and he shook it off. He broke through a fringe of brush and saw what claimed their attention.

A cow was bogged down in a fast-drying hole. Only a little water remained, and the gray, adhesive mud stretched all around her. She had torn up a lot of the mud in an effort to free herself, but now she was passive but still bright-eyed and alert, her head turning to watch Ashel's progress. She hadn't given up. He could tell by the lift of her head. If she were in there too long, she would become convinced she could not move, and even if she were dragged to firmer land, she would make no effort to stand.

Cabe was shaking out his rope. "If Pete and I get a rope on her, can you tail her up?"

Ashel nodded. He had to wade into the mud, twist and lift on the cow's tail. It was a messy job, but he was the logical one for it. He doubted he could place a loop over her horns, if he tried all day.

The mud was soft and holding, reaching halfway up his thighs. She struggled as he came toward her, and he could hear the gooey sucking of the mud as she tried to free her hoofs. Cabe's loop settled over her horns, then Pete's.

"Now," Cabe yelled.

The horses moved away, and the ropes tightened. Ashel had hold of her tail, lifting as much as he could. He could hear the horses' choppy breathing as they dug in their hoofs for more purchase. He breathed hard with the strain of his efforts. At first he thought she was mired fast, then slowly she began to move toward dryer ground, bawling in wild-eyed protest.

The rate of progress quickened, and Ashel lost his hold

on her tail, almost falling forward into the mud. It didn't matter now. The horses would be able to drag her clear. The cow's neck was stretched like a bowstring, and it was a wonder it could withstand the awful pressure put upon it.

Ashel followed her out of the mud. He grinned at Cabe and Pete, expecting to share a moment. The three of them had saved a cow.

Cabe and Pete cast off their loops and backed their horses. The cow lay on her side, breathing heavily, her eyes still rolling. She rolled over and found that her legs still responded. She got them under her, heaved her rear end skyward, and stood.

She glared about her, seeking someone to punish for the indignities she suffered. She could not punish the men on horseback; she could not even catch them. But the man on foot— Ah, that was different.

She whirled and charged Ashel. He stood on dry ground, using the edge of his palm in trying to slice some of the sticky mud from his clothing.

The sound of the cow's charge jerked his head around. Alarm tightened his face. Blackie was too far away to reach. Already those ugly horns were close. He knew he couldn't out-foot her. There was only one place for him to go. He turned and ran a half-dozen steps back toward the mudhole and dived into it, face down. He hit with a smack, and even though his mouth was closed, mud forced its way into it.

He twisted and stood, and he was a mess. He was covered with mud from head to foot. The stuff was in his hair, his eyes, his mouth. He knuckled his eyes clean and looked around for the cow.

She stood at the edge of the mudhole, bawling and pawing the ground. She had been in that mud once, and that was enough. She bawled a final defiance at Ashel, then returned and trotted off into the brush.

Cabe and Pete were bent over in their saddles as they laughed. Wave after wave of their uncontrollable laughter hit Ashel like slaps in the face. Cabe knew that cow had been bogged down; he had probably seen her earlier in the day. And he had led Ashel to this spot, knowing what the results would be.

"God-damn you," Ashel screamed at them. He strode out of the mud toward them. He had no clear idea of what he was going to do. He was too enraged to think clearly.

Cabe lifted his head and looked beyond Ashel. He said something to Pete and both men turned their horses and spurred away. Ashel looked around, and Vaughan was riding toward him.

He pulled up beside Ashel, and his expression was not amused. "What happened?"

"Cabe sent me in to tail up a cow. She put me back in the mud." Ashel shook with his anger.

Vaughan stared after Cabe with narrowed eyes. "Dandy is getting real cute. He knew what that cow was going to do. It's up to the riders to haze a cow away from a man coming out of a bog. You hit the only spot that was safe." His eyes turned bleak. "Maybe Dandy figured on you not knowing where to go. Mount up. We're going to catch Dandy and let him clean some mud off you."

Ashel's anger was cooling. What Vaughan proposed would make matters worse. Ashel was willing to let it stop here, to let Cabe have his laugh. He looked at Vaughan's set expression. No one was going to argue Milo out of this.

He mounted, having trouble with Blackie. No horse liked to see an apparent chunk of the earth walking at him.

They spurred after Cabe and Pete and saw them split, each very intent on pursuing their business. Cabe was chasing a steer, and Vaughan followed him. Cabe knew Vaughan's temper in this, and he hoped to stay clear until it weakened.

The steer dodged and twisted, and Cabe's mare stuck to it. Every now and then Cabe looked around to see if Vaughan was slackening off.

It happened while he was looking over his shoulder. The mare stepped into a hole and went down heavily. Cabe must have kicked his feet free of the stirrups as she started her fall, for he half jumped and was half thrown over her head. He lit hard, and his face skidded for several feet along the ground.

Ashel expected him to be knocked unconscious, but Cabe was sitting up by the time they reached him. He turned to the mare and let Vaughan go to Cabe.

The mare threshed about on the ground. Each time she attempted to rise, a foreleg buckled under her. Ashel was sickened by the sight of that foreleg. The bone was snapped clear through, and only the hide kept the dangling hoof in place.

The side of Cabe's face was scraped raw. The stunned look was leaving his eyes, and he looked back at his horse. "Is Jenny all right?" he asked huskily.

Vaughan shook his head. "You got more than you bargained for, Dandy. I'll send a horse back for you." He turned away without further rebuke. All the words in the world couldn't have heaped more on Cabe than he was carrying.

For a moment, Ashel thought Cabe was talking about Jenobia, Vaughan's daughter, then he realized Cabe had named the mare Jenny. He could not believe it, but there were tears in Cabe's eyes.

He forgave Cabe a lot in that moment. When a man loved a horse, he had a right to cry when something like this happened.

He said in a low voice, "Dandy, I'm sorry."

Cabe stared at him, and Ashel thought, he doesn't even hear me. Then those eyes turned wild behind their sheen of tears. "Get away from here." Cabe had trouble with his words. "Goddamn you," he said savagely. "You won't always be working for Milo."

Ashel mounted Blackie and joined Vaughan. Vaughan's face was set, and Ashel thought, he's suffering for Cabe, too. Neither looked around at the thin sound of a shot.

CHAPTER NINE

Paw said, "I'll guess you'll be home for good tomorrow night."

Ashel nodded. Tomorrow was his last day at the M swinging V. He hated for the month to end for several reasons. He would miss the Vaughans, he would miss the food. Then there would be the loss of security by being there. Cabe never spoke to him since the mare broke her leg, but each time he looked at Ashel, there was a savage promise in his eyes. The promise said: Wait until you leave here. Ashel thought a lot about it, and it scared him.

He said, "I came home tonight to take Lady back with me in the morning." He would miss Blackie, too, and a sudden, sickening longing was in him.

Paw said, "I'm glad you're coming back, Ashel. Things just don't go right when you're not around. You know we didn't get all the wheat in."

Anger tightened Ashel's face. They got very little of the wheat in. It meant another bad year, a year of more grinding poverty. The wheat in the country looked good. This could have been a good year for this family, too.

Paw said in an aggrieved voice, "You don't know what's happened to us. The harness broke, then Nellie was sick. Hobe and Nobby were sick, too." His hands lifted and fell in a helpless gesture. "The time just slipped by. Sometimes, it's more than a man can bear."

"Sure, Paw." Anger at him was useless. It would always be this way.

Paw's face brightened at Ashel's lack of anger. He fell into step with him. "I don't know how we're going to get through the year."

Ashel didn't, either. Unless they hired out to somebody. He thought grimly, and that includes Paw and Hobe and Nobby.

He lay awake a long time that night. He would be making his last ride to the M swinging V tomorrow. It had a lonely, desolate ring.

Vaughan was at the barn when Ashel rode up in the morning. Ashel led Lady, and Vaughan looked at her. "Why the extra horse?"

Ashel frowned at him. Vaughan knew why he brought

Lady. "I wasn't planning on walking home tonight."

Vaughan seemed in high spirits, and Ashel thought dolefully, maybe he's glad to be rid of me.

Vaughan waited until Ashel put away the horses. "Your month's up."

Ashel nodded. A lot of words were choked up in his throat.

Vaughan reached into his pocket. "I've got something for you." He counted out forty dollars into Ashel's hand.

He stared at Vaughan, confusion in his eyes.

Vaughan's grin grew more broad. "Your wages, boy."

Ashel shook his head. "I didn't earn any money. I paid out that steer." He tried to hand the money back to Vaughan.

Vaughan brushed his hand aside. "You're taking it. Look at this place. You did twice what I expected. And Millie's been off my back. You earned double money. Half of it the steer and half of it money."

Ashel continued to shake his head, and Vaughan scowled at him. "You're one of those kind who has to have everything one sided. You don't want to let another man feel like he's returning as much as he gets." He threw his arm across Ashel's shoulders. "You earned it, Ashel. Both Millie and I are grateful."

Ashel turned his head. He didn't want Vaughan seeing him looking like this.

Vaughan asked, "How'd you like to work here steady?"

Ashel's eyes were incredulous, and Vaughan nodded. "I mean it, Ashel. You don't have to give me your answer now. Think about it."

Forty dollars coming in every month. Why, it would be a

fortune to a family in need. That amount monthly would carry a family through to next year, when a new crop could be planted. He said, "If you're sure you want me—"

Vaughan's face creased in a pleased smile. "Now, I don't have to face Millie and tell her you're leaving."

He lifted his voice and called to the house, "Millie, you about ready?"

She called back some garbled reply, and Vaughan said, "That means she isn't. Come along with us into town. Maybe you'd like to pick up some things."

Ashel's hand closed around the money in his pocket. He needed clothes. My God, how he needed them. But his family also needed that money. He sighed and said, "I guess there's nothing I really need."

Vaughan had a sly look on his face. "We heard from Jenny yesterday. She'll be home the first of the week."

Her picture sprang vividly into Ashel's mind. He thought of her seeing him in these worn-out clothes, and his face felt hot. He said, "Maybe there are a few things I need in town."

Vaughan did not smile. "Good. We'll start in fifteen minutes. If I can get Millie moving."

Ashel climbed into the buckboard behind them. Millie asked, "Did Milo tell you Jenny is coming?" At Ashel's nod, she said, "I'm so excited I can hardly talk."

Vaughan grunted. "They never made a woman that excited." He threw up his arm as though he feared a blow.

Millie merely sniffed. "He thinks he's awfully funny."

Ashel settled down for the bumpy ride into town. Those two had a good life together. He carefully kept from comparing his family with the Vaughans. Some had a good life, some didn't. He let it go at that.

He kept touching the money in his pocket. He was going to spend a major part of it on himself, and he supposed he should be feeling guilt, but he did not. If he was going to work for Vaughan, he needed clothes. Buying the clothes now meant that the family would get all his pay during the summer. What he spent today was a good investment for them. He grinned at his reasoning. A man could argue black was white, if he wanted it that way.

Vaughan drove into town and stopped before Atkins' General Store. He tied the reins to the rack and said, "We'll meet you here in an hour, Ashel. Will that give you enough time?"

Ashel nodded and said, "Plenty." Excitement was growing in him. He was in town with money to spend, to spend as he wished. He could walk into any store along this street and return stare for stare. Money made a difference in a man's outlook.

He watched Millie and Vaughan move away. Good people, he thought with a rush of emotion.

He climbed the two steps to Atkins' porch and opened the door. Atkins was waiting on two women. He looked up at Ashel's entrance, and his eyes were indifferent.

Ashel knew that look. It said, here was a customer with little or no money to spend. He thought, I'll change that look.

He wandered about the store, while Atkins finished with the women. Atkins was a miserable storekeeper. He had hardware mixed with dry goods, patent medicine in with his food stuffs. The town dust coated everything. Each time a rider or a wagon stirred it in the street, more of it drifted in here.

Ashel thought the two women would never finish their buying. They finally left, and Atkins stayed behind the counter. He was a sour, grizzled man with a growing paunch that he rested on the countertops whenever possible.

"What do you want?" His voice was hostile.

"Some clothing." Ashel had already picked out his items. Two pairs of Levi's, two work shirts, a pair of boots and a hat, and neither of the last two items could be expensive. If he could squeeze it all in, he wanted a dress shirt.

Atkins grunted. "No credit."

Ashel took a step toward the man, and his face was savage. He wanted to grab Atkins, jerk him from behind his counter, and rub his nose raw with the money in his pocket. He controlled himself. He was working for Vaughan now, and anything he did would come right back on Vaughan.

"I'm not asking for credit." He pulled the money from his pocket and saw the change in Atkins' face. The penny-rubbing bastard, he thought. He should walk out of here, but he needed those clothes, and Atkins was the best place in town to get them.

He bought the Levi's and work shirts, ignoring Atkins' attempt at conversation. He rejected a pair of boots because of their cost and selected a serviceable work pair. He liked the feel of the expensive hats, but cost had a hard grip on the back of his neck. He bought a cheap hat and said recklessly, "I'll take that dress shirt." It was green with fancy buttons. It wouldn't wear worth a damn, but it was pretty.

He asked, "Can I change here?"

Atkins was eager to please him. He said, "In the back room." He moistened the stub of a pencil and added up the total. It came to thirty-four dollars and a few cents.

Ashel stuffed the change into his pocket. It shot hell out of the forty dollars. He would give what was left to Paw. Next month the family would get all of it. The guilt feeling wasn't very strong.

He changed to the new clothes and chose the dress shirt over the work shirts. It wouldn't hurt just to wear it back to the ranch. He creased and cocked the new hat and tried to see himself in the hand mirror, tacked to the wall. The mirror was wavy and flyspecked. He thought he looked fine.

He started to throw away the old clothes, then changed his mind. He could still get a little service out of them. He rolled everything in a piece of newspaper and tucked the bulky bundle under his arm.

He felt self-conscious as he walked toward the front door. The new boots pinched his little toes. But they would loosen with wear.

"Come back," Atkins called after him.

Ashel did not acknowledge the invitation. Sure, Atkins wanted him to come back—when he had money again.

He walked outside and placed his bundles in the buck-board. He leaned against a wheel, waiting for Milo and Millie.

This was a weekday, and there wasn't much traffic in town. A rider drifted by, and he did not look at Ashel. At least, the new clothes gave him security from that angle. They didn't stamp him as a sodbuster. The homesteaders would look at these clothes with different eyes, hostile eyes. He thought glumly, a man cannot walk the middle. He's forced to one side or the other.

He didn't hear Cassie until she spoke to him. He turned, and his face was filled with delight at the sight of her. His face sobered as a guilty thought crept into his mind. He wasn't thinking of Cassie, when he came into town to buy these clothes.

The laughter was gone from her eyes as she looked at him. She said, "I saw you every time you passed the house. You didn't try to stop."

He stiffened at the accusation in her voice. "You heard what Clell said."

"You could've gotten word to me some way. I'd have met you any place you wanted."

He said miserably, "Aw, Cassie." Couldn't she understand there were some situations a man couldn't fight? He stared at her. She was still pretty. But it was a kind of immature prettiness. Not like Jenny's at all. He thought gloomily, if just a picture could make this much difference, there never was much between us.

She said, "You're different, someway."

"I bought some new clothes."

"It's more than that," she said slowly.

He couldn't think of anything to say. It's not my fault, he thought half angrily. Clell Reynolds slammed the door between us. He wished the Vaughans would come back.

It was almost a relief, when Reynolds came across the street. No one had to take a second look to see how mad Reynolds was.

He stepped onto the walk and said, "Cassie, didn't I tell you not to talk to him again?"

She said, "If he wants me to talk to him, I'll talk to him."

Ashel gave her a surprised glance. He didn't know she had that much spirit.

Reynolds turned on him with a bitter look in his eyes. He took in the new clothes and said, "It's easy to see where you stand."

Ashel made a last attempt to pacify him. "Clell, because I'm working for Vaughan doesn't—"

Reynolds stabbed a finger at Ashel's face, cutting him short. "If you're working for him, you're taking his orders. If he tells you to turn against your kind, even your own family, you'll do it."

Reynolds was beyond the reach of reasoning words. Ashel said in disgust, "Of all the damned nonsense."

"Is it?" Reynolds yelled. "I'll show you others feel the same way."

Cassie's face was distressed. She moved to her father and tugged on his arm. "Please. Everyone in town will hear you."

"I want them to." Reynolds raised his voice to two men just coming out of a store across the street. "Abe. Suge. Come over here."

Abe Milton and Suge Thomas crossed the street, their faces curious.

Reynolds pointed at Ashel. "Look at him. Tell him where you think he belongs."

Their faces darkened as they stared at Ashel. "He looks like one of them," Thomas grunted.

"He is. He's working for Vaughan. Some night, at Vaughan's orders, he'll be riding out to put a torch to your barn."

"God-damn it, Clell," Ashel yelled, "that's crazy talk, and you know it."

"Is it?" Reynolds thrust his face close to Ashel's. "I say you're ready to turn against your own family."

Other men drifted to the scene, pulled by the loud voices. Ashel saw Brosnahan, Slezak, and Wenski. A few days ago he would have called these men friends. Now they listened to Reynolds, and the blackness grew in their faces, saying they were not friends now.

Ashel was hemmed in by a ring of hostile faces. He was too angry to know fear. All of them were as bad as Reynolds. They accused without proof. He said, "If you knew Milo Vaughan, you'd know how wrong you are. I don't know who's behind the trouble, but Milo has no hand in it."

He saw them look at each other and nod. The nods didn't clear Vaughan. They only implicated Ashel.

"He's joined them all right," Milton said. "Maybe we ought to show him how we feel. Maybe we ought to take those fancy clothes off him right here."

Ashel saw the idea grow in their eyes. These were embittered men, roughed up by adversities and their struggle against a hostile land. They needed something tangible to blame, and it stood before them.

"Stop it," Cassie cried. Her voice fell on unhearing ears.

Ashel was backed against the buckboard wheel. If he made a move to break through them, they would jump him like a pack of hungry dogs. He wished he had a club. He balled his fists and said savagely, "Try it."

"He's asking for it," Reynolds said.

The first shuffling motion wasn't a full step, but it was

movement toward Ashel. He braced himself for a forward push off the wheel. Slezak was the smallest. If Ashel could hit and break through him—

Then he heard an angry voice roar, "Hold it. What the hell's going on here?"

Ashel turned his head, and Vaughan and Millie came down the walk. Vaughan threw out a hand, stopping her, and came on. He pushed through the ring of men and stood beside Ashel. "What is this?" he demanded.

Relief made Ashel's knees feel loose. Once these men were his friends, and he still tried to save the situation. "Just a misunderstanding, Milo."

"No misunderstanding," Reynolds bellowed. "We understand too well."

Vaughan's eyes were piercing. "What does that mean, Reynolds?"

The full impact of those cold eyes hit Reynolds, and he shifted uneasily. He said doggedly, "He's with you now."

"What's wrong with that?"

Reynolds squirmed on the pinpoint of those eyes. Vaughan was a big man, and Reynolds was not yet ready to brace him.

"He's part of the trouble we've been having," Reynolds said. "We know you want us out of the country."

Vaughan's eyes swept from face to face. "You crazy fools," he said contemptuously, "I don't give a damn what you do. Just don't bother me or my men. If I wanted you out of the country, I wouldn't have to do a thing. The country would run you out by itself." He grew angrier with each word. "You don't belong here in the first place. You come in here and plow up good grass land—" He checked himself and breathed hard.

Reynolds looked at his friends. It was a knowing look, saying, "See!"

Vaughan caught the look and its implications. His anger was back in full force. "Believe what you want to," he said flatly. "If you want trouble now, you can have it."

He stood beside Ashel, a big man, his eyes darkened with anger.

Indecision was on their faces. This was a different matter than a few moments ago.

"I thought so," Vaughan said. "Clear away from my buckboard."

They gave before his eyes, opening up the walk.

"Millie," Vaughan called. "Come on."

Ashel glanced at Cassie as he climbed into the buckboard. Her face was white, and he was positive tears were in her eyes.

Vaughan untied the team and settled himself beside Millie. He looked at the men and said, "Don't bother him again." He slapped the reins against the team's rumps, putting them into motion.

Reynolds yelled after them, "If you try to see Cassie again, I'll blow your head off."

Ashel stared straight ahead. He didn't intend to try to see Cassie again.

Millie looked at him, and there was worry in her eyes. "Don't worry," she said. "He's just angry now." She sighed as she drew no response. "She's a pretty girl."

Ashel wanted to yell at her, don't talk like that. She's not my girl. At least, she's not now.

CHAPTER TEN

Ashel dropped Blackie's reins and led Lady into the shed. He came out, and Paw said, "We could've used her today. If you're working for Vaughan steady, there was no need in taking her this morning."

Ashel said patiently, "I told you I didn't know it this morning." He debated upon giving the five dollars to Paw and decided against it. It would be better to give the money to his mother.

Paw's eyes brightened. "Forty dollars a month. That's going to come in right handy for us, Ashel. I don't know how we'd pulled through without it. I wish he'd paid you for the first month."

"He did," Ashel said shortly. "I had to have some clothes."

Paw shook his head. "I was wondering where you got them." His eyes were envious as he swept Ashel from head to toe. "It don't seem hardly fair, Ashel. You spending all that money when we need so many things."

It was hard for Ashel to keep a leash on his patience. He moved toward the house and said over his shoulder as Paw started to follow him, "I want to talk to Maw alone."

Paw leaned against the shed wall, his face sullen. "You don't have to tell me anything. I'm only your Paw."

Ashel moved toward the house without answering. He was glad Hobe and Nobby were not around. The three of them jawing at him would have been too much.

Elodia was just coming out of the house, and Ashel stopped her. He led her around the corner and pressed a half dollar into her hand.

Her eyes grew wider and wider as she looked at it. "Is it all mine?" she whispered.

He rubbed his knuckles across her forehead. "All yours. You hide it, then when you're in town, you buy yourself something you want. Don't tell them anything about it," he warned.

"I won't." A wisdom was in her eyes, a wisdom too soon learned.

"It's our secret, Ashel." She threw her arms about his chest. "Oh, Ashel. Ashel."

He didn't want her crying. He disengaged her arms. "Here now. Quit that. Go find a good place to hide it."

He watched her run away. She would change that hiding place a half hundred times, knowing a delicious savoring each time she handled the coin.

He walked into the house, and the same old disorder was there. His mother looked up from the stove, and her eyes quickened with interest at sight of him. "My, you look nice. Those are new clothes, aren't they?"

He caught no rebuke in her voice. He nodded and said, "Vaughan paid me for the month I just put in. He didn't have to."

"He sounds like a good man."

Ashel nodded again. "He wants me to work steady for him." He pulled out the five dollars and laid it in her hand. "That's all that's left this month, Maw. But next month, you'll have it all." Maybe he would keep a dollar or two for himself but no more.

He suspected it had been a long time since she had held that much money. Tears filled her eyes, and she said,

"You're a good boy, Ashel."

Her eyes were furtive as she glanced toward the door. "Does Paw know?"

"No. Neither does Hobe nor Nobby. It's all yours, Maw. Don't tell them about it."

Her hand was in her apron pocket, and he knew it clutched the money. "I won't." She sounded determined.

He started for the door, and she cried, "You're staying for supper."

He shook his head. "I can't. I promised Vaughan I'd be back early." That wasn't true, but it would excuse him. It was odd how uncomfortable he felt here any more. He thought soberly, I'm a stranger in my own home.

She hurried to the door to catch him and pleaded, "You'll be back soon?"

"I'll be back." He bent and kissed her forehead. He felt the fierce asking in her hands as she clutched his arm. "Don't worry, Maw. Things are going to be better."

"We could be standing it." Her tone said she did not believe it.

He hoped the money would give her the same lift it gave Elodia. He walked toward the shed, making a mental vow. He would see that things were better for her.

Hobe and Nobby were standing beside Blackie when Ashel reached the shed. His face went wooden. He had hoped he could leave before they returned.

Hobe's eyes were mean as he looked at Ashel. "Paw said you were walking around all duded up. Spent all of it on yourself, didn't you? You don't give a damn about Maw and Elodia."

Ashel's temper boiled. Hobe was a fine one to talk like

this. "I never noticed you doing anything for them."

Nobby had an evil grin. "The new clothes makes him talk kind of sassy, Hobe. He oughta have a little money in his pockets. Let's look and see."

Paw squalled, "Stop it. You hear me? I won't have any trouble between you." He might have as well shouted at the wind.

Hobe and Nobby edged toward him, and Ashel read the intent in their faces. They carried a grudge, and they thought now was as good a time as any to settle it.

He said, "Keep your hands off me."

They thought the tightness in his voice was fear. Nobby grinned at Hobe. "We won't touch him, if he turns his pockets out, will we, Hobe?"

"He needs a beating," Hobe growled. "That's a right pretty shirt he's wearing. I might just take it." He laid a hand on Ashel's arm.

Ashel struck it away. He had two of them, and they had beaten him before. But that was when he accepted their authority.

Hobe looked surprised, then the meanness came back. "Why, you damned fool," he said softly.

He bounded forward and swung a clubbing blow at Ashel. Ashel ducked, and the fist slid over his shoulder. He hit Hobe in the belly, knocking him back and jerking an explosive grunt from him. He whirled, and Nobby was rushing him. He jolted him in the face, and Nobby yelled. Ashel hit that open mouth, and Nobby's teeth broke skin on his hand. Nobby fell into him, his hands open and clawing. One of them fastened on Ashel's sleeve. Ashel felt the pulling weight of it, then he heard the rip of material. He threw Nobby from him and looked at the sleeve. It was torn free at the shoulder, and the length of it dangled about his wrist. He sobbed with rage as he jerked the ruined sleeve from his arm. This was a brand new shirt, worn less than a day. Its damage enraged him far beyond any hurt they could give him.

"Come on," he panted. "I'll beat your heads off."

"Stop it," Paw yelled. "Stop it."

No one gave him a glance.

Hobe was still recovering from the hurt in his belly, and Nobby ran a hand across his split lips. He looked wonderingly at the blood on it and said, "Hobe, he's gone purely crazy."

Hobe moved forward again, but this time more cautiously. "We'll knock some of that craziness out of him," he growled.

Ashel didn't wait for them to reach him. He leaped forward and sledged Nobby in the chest. Nobby's face was pained as he slowly sat down. Ashel turned to see where Hobe was, and something hard landed on his cheekbone. It knocked him back a step, and he momentarily lost his vision. He shook his head to clear it and charged Hobe. Hobe was awkward and unskilled, and he faced a rage beyond his knowledge. He retreated before an avalanche of blows, his arms trying to cover his face. Ashel knocked him down and looked for Nobby.

"Get up, Nobby," Hobe yelled. "Get up and stop him."

Paw screeched and danced up and down. None of the three heard what he was saying.

Nobby crawled to a broken piece of two-by-four. It was almost three feet long, and one end was splintered. It made an ugly weapon. His hand closed on it, and he got to his feet. "I got me a club, Hobe," he yelled. His teeth were bared as he faced Ashel. "Now, goddamn you," he said and moved slowly toward Ashel.

Ashel let him come to him. He timed the blow right, waiting until it was swinging at him. He crouched and jerked his head aside, and the club went over his shoulder. He felt it rap against his back. The momentum of the swing pulled Nobby into him, and Ashel got his shoulder under his breastbone. He straightened, lifting him, and Nobby hollered. He dropped the club, and his nails clawed at Ashel's back. Ashel heard material rip again.

He spun and heaved Nobby from him, and he was close enough to the shed that he flung Nobby into it. Nobby's head hit the boards. His eyes showed mostly white, and he made a coughing *Aggrahh*. He slid down to the base of the shed, landing in a sitting position, his head hanging on his chest. For a moment, he looked as though he were asleep, then slowly, he toppled over. He sprawled loosely in the dust, his face turned up. Ashel saw the rasp of his breathing through slack lips.

He whirled to find Hobe, and Hobe was up on one knee. Hobe made a sound that was half sob and half rage. He and Nobby had handled Ashel before without a tenth of this trouble. And now look what had happened. Nobby was out cold, and he was pretty battered.

He looked about for a weapon, and his hand closed on a rock. He could stop that damned Ashel with this. He could knock him right off his feet. His arm came back for the throw as Ashel rushed at him.

Ashel never let Hobe let go with the rock. He lifted and

rammed his knee into Hobe's jaw, and Hobe spilled over on his back. He let out a long, gusty sigh, twitched a couple of times, and was still.

A sleeve of Ashel's shirt was gone, and he knew most of the back must be, too, for he could feel the breeze on his bare skin. His eyes filled with hot, stinging tears, enraged tears.

Paw looked from Hobe to Nobby. His voice was filled with awe and accusation. "Look what you done. You oughta be ashamed. Doing something like that to your brothers."

Ashel faced him. In the gathering darkness, he didn't realize what a menacing appearance he made. Paw retreated a step. "It's a pretty awful thing, when a man's sons fight like this."

It was useless to point out who had started this fight. Ashel moved past his father toward Blackie. He picked up the reins and threw them across Blackie's neck. He mounted and rode past his father.

"Ashel," Paw yelled. "You come back here and help me with Hobe and Nobby. You hear me, Ashel?"

Ashel quickened Blackie's pace. He would come here as rarely as he could. Not because he was afraid of Hobe and Nobby. Because he was afraid of himself. He thought glumly, if Reynolds hears of this, it'll confirm all his suspicions. Ashel had turned against his family.

He gingerly touched his right eye, and swore as he felt its sensitive swelling. If it wasn't closed by morning, it would at least be discolored. And Jenobia was coming home tomorrow.

He put Blackie away in Vaughan's barn and moved

toward the bunkhouse, hoping no one was there. He stepped inside, and Tom and Lanny looked at him.

Tom said, "My God. You been in another one?"

Lanny's voice was filled with satisfaction. "From the looks of it I'd say he took a beating."

Tom said scornfully, "You don't see very well. That doesn't look like any whipped look in his face." He asked hopefully, "Who got in an argument with you boy?" He didn't really expect an answer.

Lanny said, "I'd judge it was someone who objected to him trying to look like a cowman."

Ashel's eye and a half blazed at him. "You want to try to take the rest of this shirt off me?"

Lanny tried to meet that stare, then his eyes broke, and he looked away. Tom's dry chuckle didn't help matters any.

Lanny swore and got to his feet. He walked to the door, then turned. He leveled a finger at Ashel and said, "Milo won't be backing you all the time." It was a sad, little effort to salvage something, and Lanny knew it. He stalked off into the night.

Tom chuckled again. "He's not about to give you more than words. He remembers that fracas you had with Dandy." He critically inspected Ashel's swelling eye. "That's going to be a real beaut by morning. You pick up knocks like a dog picks up fleas." He pulled a bandanna from his hip pocket. "Maybe a cold rag will help the swelling some. Or I could go to the house for a piece of steak. But Millie's going to ask questions."

Ashel shook his head.

"Thought you'd feel that way." Tom stepped outside, and Ashel heard the slosh of water from the bucket as Tom wet the bandanna. He came back and said, "Hold this to your eye. You're going to be real pretty when Miss Jenny gets here."

Ashel's face twisted with such a raw, violent expression that Tom backed. "Here now," he said. "I was only funning you."

He watched Ashel stretch out on his bunk and hold the wet cloth to his eye. Some people attracted hard knocks. Maybe Ashel was one of those kinds. He thought of Ashel's look when he said Miss Jenny's name, and mentally shook his head. Ashel could be asking for another hard knock—a real bad one this time.

CHAPTER ELEVEN

Ashel was first out of the bunkhouse in the morning. And he did not go to the house for breakfast. He busied himself in the big barn and heard Millie call him several times. The last time impatience was in her voice, and he knew she would not wait longer on him.

This was a big day for the M swinging V. After breakfast all of them were riding to town to meet Jenobia. Millie and Milo expected Ashel to join them, but he wasn't going. It was all right for Tom and Dandy and the others. They knew Jenobia. Ashel didn't. And besides, he had a very black eye.

Fifteen minutes later, he heard Millie call him again and suspected they were ready to leave.

Vaughan's voice came so unexpectedly that Ashel jumped. It sounded right outside the barn door, and he stepped back into an obscure corner. "Dandy," Vaughan asked, "have you seen Ashel?"

"No," Cabe said curtly.

"I don't know where the hell he could be," Vaughan said. "Millie wanted us all to go to welcome Jenny. She'll be hollering at us next. We'd better be moving."

"You ride on ahead, Milo." Cabe's voice sounded odd. "I've got something to do. I'll catch up with you."

"Don't be long," Vaughan warned. "Millie's upset enough about Ashel."

The sound of one set of footsteps drifted away. The sound of the other seemed to be coming toward the barn door. That would be Cabe, Ashel thought, and he shrank farther back into his corner. He felt his face tighten. Was Cabe looking for him? If he was, it wouldn't be for anything pleasant.

He could hear Cabe's movements inside the barn and dared not look. But the sound seemed away from him and more toward the box stalls. He wished he knew what Cabe was doing.

The sound of laughter carried to him from the direction of the house. This was a holiday, and they were skylarking around. By the volume of the final whoop, he guessed they were on the way. Loneliness hit him like a club. He wished he was going with them.

He risked a quick look to see what Cabe was doing. Cabe stood in the doorway of the barn, his head cocked in a listening attitude. Cabe, too, was apparently waiting for them to leave.

He carried a huge bunch of flowers in his right hand, and Ashel had never seen his face look quite like this. He tried to put a description to it, and it suddenly came to him.

Cabe's face had a soft look.

He waited a long time after Cabe left the barn. He suspected that anyone seeing Cabe with that bunch of flowers would catch hell.

He walked toward the house and entered the kitchen. He was sure he knew where those flowers were, but he wanted to see for himself. He moved to the room, where he fixed the window, and looked into it. Cabe's flowers were in a bowl beside Jenobia's picture. A drop of moisture glistened on one of the petals like a miniature jewel. Cabe had evidently gotten up early this morning, gathered those flowers, then placed them beside the picture after the others left.

A dozen different kinds of wild flowers were in the bowl. Ashel recognized the delicate glacier lilies, the alpine poppies, and the columbine. Cabe had ridden into high country for those. The brilliant orange of Indian paintbrush blended with asters and arnicas. Ashel did not know the others.

He looked from the flowers to the picture. The flowers would delight any woman's heart, and he wished he had thought of them. He knew a sudden baseless anger and was tempted to hurl the bowl of flowers through the open window. He turned abruptly and left the room.

He heard them return in midafternoon. He stayed stubbornly on his ladder, replacing the rotting facer board at the rear of the barn. Holding the long board in place to get a nail started and keeping his balance on the ladder at the same time was a ticklish task. He dropped a nail and swore. He fumbled for another and got it started. He drove it in with savage licks. He would work out here until dark. He wouldn't go to the house at all. He knew when an outsider should stay away. He also recognized self-pity, and he drove in the next nail with even more vicious licks, denting the board with the hammer head.

He could reach no farther without moving his ladder, and he started to climb down.

"Hello there," a voice said.

He knew who it was without turning his head. The girl of the picture would have such a voice, light and bright and with overtones of laughter in it.

She stared up at him. The picture didn't do her justice. His heart bucked worse than Blackie ever could, and for an instant, his tongue wouldn't move.

"Hello," he said gruffly.

"Are you glued up there?"

"I guess not," he said and slowly descended. He thought of the ruined dress shirt with regret.

She was taller than his mental picture of her. The crown of her hair came to the bridge of his nose. A man could be fooled by the soft, feminine look of her until he looked at her eyes. They were deep, assured eyes, and they weighed a man better than a pair of scales.

He realized she was staring at his bruised eye, and color flooded his face. Laughter bubbled in her eyes, and she fought against it.

"Go on. Laugh," he growled.

The first peal escaped before she could cover her mouth with her hand.

His expression was injured and indignant. She choked off her laughter and said, "I'm sorry, Ashel." She placed her fingers on his arm. "I couldn't say it's becoming, could I?"

His sense of humor saved him, and he admitted, "I guess not."

Her smile had the ability to make a man go all loose inside. "I'm Jenny."

"I knew by your picture." His tone carried admiration, putting color into her face. "How did you know my name?"

"Millie wrote about you. She told me what you'd done around here. I never saw the place looking this well."

His heart pounded at a furious, uneven beat. She knew all about him, and she had looked him up. The implication was dazzling, then a sharp-edged thought cut through the cloud under his feet, dropping him to the ground. Don't be a damned fool, he told himself. She's being kind. No more. He said, "Millie's been good to me."

"Milo won't be, if you keep on working. Everyone's supposed to have the day off. He sent me to find you. Millie's cutting a cake in the kitchen. Aren't you going to celebrate my coming home?"

He took a deep breath and said recklessly, "Sure."

He walked with her toward the house, and the loneliness was gone.

As he entered the kitchen behind her, Cabe's eyes were upon him. They were hot and murderous, and Ashel looked away to escape them.

The kitchen was a gay and happy scene. They were glad Jenny was home, and they teased her unmercifully about some shared event in the past.

Tom took a bite of cake and said mournfully, "All that's changed now. We got a lady back here now."

Millie said crisply, "And there wasn't one around until Jenny returned."

Tom missed the sparkle in her eyes. "Aw, Millie," he protested. "You know I didn't mean that. But look at the way she's dressed. We ain't used to seeing her looking like that."

Jenny's dress matched the color of her eyes. Ashel thought she looked beautiful.

Jenny said, "I can fix that." She was gone fifteen minutes. When she came back, she was dressed in Levi's and a man's work shirt. Her hair was braided and hanging down her back.

Tom grinned. "Now I know you. You think you can still ride?"

"Anything," she said.

Millie and Vaughan sat and beamed at her. Their pride showed, and they had a right to it.

Ashel took no part in the conversation. He was content to just sit and watch her.

Jenny looked at him. "Milo tells me Blackie's your horse. I used to ride him."

Lanny grinned. "I remember a day a couple of years ago. He threw you pretty good that day."

His remark carried no malice, and Jenny smiled with him. "I climbed back up and rode him, didn't I?"

Cabe growled, "She was careless. She knew better. I taught her to ride."

His words brought an uncomfortable silence to the room.

Jenny's face had an odd smile. "You taught me to ride, Dandy," she agreed. "You taught me a lot of things. But the teacher wasn't always perfect. I remember Blackie throwing you."

Cabe's face flamed. She didn't say it, but her meaning was plain. Blackie had never thrown Ashel. Cabe's eyes were wicked as he looked at Ashel. He got up abruptly and left the kitchen.

"Now what's eating him?" Milo asked in astonishment.

Millie gave Jenny a sharp inquisitive glance.

Tom grinned and said, "Dandy always was a touchy man. Millie, is any more of that cake left?"

Lanny's and Pete's eyes rested on Tom in thoughtful speculation.

Ashel thought—the past minute split them. It ran a line right through the middle of this room, and a person was either on one side or the other.

He felt suddenly awkward and uncomfortable, and pushed to his feet. "I was putting up a facer board," he said. He did not look at Jenny. "I've only got a couple of nails in it. A good wind would rip it off."

He was relieved when he stepped out of the kitchen. He did not see Cabe, and that was further relief. He half expected him to be waiting outside.

In the morning, Jenny came to the barn just as Ashel finished milking. She said, "I heard about you making butter. Is there anything you can't do?"

He thought of Cabe and was uneasy. Then a surge of recklessness took him. If she wanted to talk to him, to hell with what Cabe thought.

"I guess there are a few things," he said and grinned.

"Are you too busy to go riding with me?" She made a little grimace. "Milo wants someone with me for a while.

He thinks being away has made me forget everything."

Ashel's heart accelerated. He knew there was a logical reason Milo sent her to him. He could be the most easily spared. But just the same he was going riding with her.

"Just as soon as I put the milk away." He whistled as he went toward the house.

Millie's eyes were troubled as she looked at him. "Ashel," she started, then stopped.

He said, "Yes, ma'am?" He had the feeling some sadness had touched her. It had to be a recent thing, or at least, it did not show last night.

She shook her head. "Nothing. Don't let her do anything foolish."

"No, ma'am." He was puzzled as he left the house. It sounded as though Millie were trying to tell him something and couldn't find the right words.

Jenny had the little sorrel mare almost saddled when Ashel reached the barn. He tried to help her, and she said, "Don't you start babying me."

"No," he said and stepped back to watch her. She thumped the wind out of the mare's belly and tightened the cinch another notch. She knew her way around.

The mare danced with impatience as Jenny waited for Ashel to saddle Blackie. He mounted, and Jenny cried, "Race you." She gave the mare a light lick and was off.

He spurred after her. Maybe this was what Millie meant. Riding at breakneck speed over this ground was foolish. But how could he stop her?

He fell in behind her, not trying to pass. That would only bring additional effort on her part. His fears lessened. She rode as well as a man, and he admired the give of her body

111

to the mare's motion.

She stopped at the end of a mile. Her face was flushed, her eyes shining. "Oh, Ashel. You don't know how good it is to be back."

He said gravely, "I can imagine." It was good to have her back, to feel this strong, unspoken communication. The color deepened in her face, and she looked away.

She said, "I want to show you the pool where I caught my first big trout."

They rode higher, and she called off the names of plants and trees. She pointed out limber pine and Douglas fir and western larch. Bear grass lifted its beautiful domed column of white blossoms, reaching above the Mariposa lilies, dog-tooth violets, and windflowers. She knew the yellow bell, the shooting star, and the golden aster.

He shook his head at her knowledge. He'd seen most of these growing things, but his thoughts were too occupied to seek a name for them. Now he was suddenly eager to learn.

"I know that one," he said, pointing to a plant. "That's blue cama."

She nodded. "The Indians prized it in making pemmican. I've eaten it a few times. It's not too bad. That's death cama over there. It looks a lot like blue cama. Sheepmen hate it. It's deadly to their flocks. You can usually tell it by its white blossoms."

His mouth hung slack. He mentioned the name of a flower, and she gave him a volume on it. He asked, "How did you learn so much about this stuff?"

"Dandy taught me. I've tagged after him since I was nine. He wants to know the name of everything that moves or grows."

He was sorry she brought Cabe's name into the conversation. He would never have suspected this facet of Cabe's character. He knew only the harsh, brutal side of the man. He thought, he's never given me a chance to know anything else.

He said, "He put the flowers beside your picture." He hadn't meant to say that. It just slipped out.

She gave him an odd glance. "I know. He told me."

That was a queer note in her voice, sounding almost like resentment. If he'd gathered those flowers for her, he'd never have told her.

She said abruptly, "We're almost to my pool." It sounded as though she did not want to talk about Dandy Cabe any more.

He could hear the feeble sound of the mountain stream before they reached it. They rode between pines and looked down at the pool.

Her voice was distressed as she said, "It's so low."

He shook his head. "It's been awful dry."

"It's always too dry, or too cold." She looked like Milo at the moment. "It's a bitter country, Ashel. It breaks so many people."

He soberly nodded. This was a new side he was seeing. Jenny Vaughan was aware that everything was not easy or play.

She said, "Shhh," and pointed. A dark shadow streaked through the water as a trout, disturbed by their approach, sought new sanctuary.

She turned the mare from the pool as though she found no pleasure in its sight. "Dandy was with me when I caught that big trout. I wouldn't have landed it without his help." She looked at him, and her eyes were troubled. "Why do people have to change, Ashel? When I was a kid, I wanted to be with him. I don't any more. He seems to think he owns me. It was bad last summer. And he's picked up where he left off."

He's in love with you, Jenny, Ashel thought. It probably never occurred to her, and if it did, she would deny it, an incredulous denial. Why, Dandy Cabe was almost twice her age. But age had nothing to do with a man's feelings.

"I don't know, Jenny," he said.

She looked at the sun. "We'd better be turning back." The gaiety was gone from her face.

Ashel put an oath against Cabe's name. If Cabe plagued her this summer— It was useless, finishing the thought. He didn't know what he could do about it. He turned Blackie and followed her.

Vaughan sat on the top corral bar beside Cabe and looked at the stallion. The horse thundered around the corral, bugling its fury.

"I wouldn't have that damned brute," Vaughan said. "What's he good for? Nobody's ever ridden him. He'll kill someone before he's through. I can't see why Wainright keeps him."

Cabe stared at the stallion with fascinated eyes. The horse was blood red in color, and its flowing mane and tail were black. Its little pig eyes were set in a tossing sea of muddy white, and the spike ears alternately jerked forward and back. It looked dangerous standing still, it looked even more dangerous in motion. It suddenly whirled and rushed across the corral toward Cabe's dangling boots. He kicked at its head before he jerked his feet up out of reach.

"I tried it twice," Cabe said. "He almost got me the last time." He'd never forget that attempt. He'd limped for two months after it.

He grinned at Vaughan. "I guess Travis likes to keep Fireball around because no one can ride him."

"Maybe," Vaughan grumbled. The care and feed of this animal seemed a waste to him. But some men were like that. They had to be tops, even if it came to keeping a vicious stallion. He frowned at the horse. "I wouldn't climb on him for a hundred cows. I'm not happy about keeping him even long enough for Travis to build a corral." He looked at Cabe, and his eyes were sharp.

"Fireball tore hell out of his old corral," Cabe said. "Travis was afraid the barn wouldn't hold him. I told him we had a corral that he couldn't break out of. Pete and I had a hell of a time getting him here." An aggrieved note crept into his voice. "I thought it was a neighborly thing to do. I can take him back."

"Let him stay," Vaughan said. He squinted at the sun. "Jenny and Ashel should be getting back."

Cabe's voice was casual. "Where'd they go?"

"Up in the hills someplace." Vaughan did not see the twitch in Cabe's face. He stared toward the northwest and said, "I think that's them coming now."

Both men were silent as they watched the riders approach. Had Vaughan been watching Cabe he would have seen the wicked fire grow in his eyes.

They climbed down from the corral as Jenny and Ashel neared the barn. Vaughan uncinched the saddle for his daughter and asked, "Have a good ride?"

"We rode up to the pool." Jenny looked at Cabe. "You know the one, Dandy. Where you helped me catch the trout."

"I remember." Cabe's words sounded forced.

Jenny turned her head at the squealing and snorting that came from the corral. "What's that?"

Vaughan said, "We've got to keep Fireball until Wainright can build a new corral."

Jenny looked at Ashel. "I'll show you the most beautiful horse you ever saw. And the meanest."

The four of them climbed back to the top bar. Fireball rushed at them, veered off just before he smashed into the bars, and raced around the enclosure.

Jenny said, "He makes me shiver just to look at him. Dandy, did anybody ride him while I was away?"

The cords in Cabe's neck stood out like small cables. "Nobody will ever ride him," he said.

"They can't, if you can't," she agreed. "I remember the last time you tried. I thought I'd die before you got out."

Cabe shook his head. "He's too much horse for any man."

Ashel couldn't keep his eyes off the animal. He had never seen such a piece of horseflesh in his life. He recognized the animal's menace, but its challenge was a stronger pull. He had been thrown before, several times. But he always came back and broke his animal. Could he ride this one? The question grew larger in his mind. It pried at him with strong, insistent fingers, wanting to be answered. Cabe, by his own admission, hadn't been able to ride him. What if Ashel were able to tame this brute, what if he could do what no one else could do? And with Jenny looking on— He drew a deep breath and said, "I'd like to try him." He wasn't really conscious of saying those words, but there they were for everyone to hear.

Vaughan said explosively, "You damned fool. Haven't you been listening? No one's ridden him."

"You can't," Jenny cried. Her face carried lines of strain.

Cabe said grudgingly, "That kind of talk takes guts." He shook his head. "If I couldn't do it, you can't."

Ashel couldn't back out now. His jaw had a stubborn set. "I'd like to try." A man wanted standing in a woman's eyes.

Vaughan swore at him and said, "I won't let you. You don't know what you're getting into."

"I know," Ashel said, his breathing faster. He felt eager excitement and a touch of fear. That was a hell of a lot of horse down there. He looked at Vaughan and said simply, "I've been thrown before."

Vaughan saw something in his eyes, and his voice was helpless. He couldn't deny Ashel his right to try if Ashel wanted it that way. "You know you're a damned fool. Take my saddle. Its newer."

Ashel nodded and climbed down from the bars. He walked toward the barn to get Vaughan's saddle. His knees had a funny kind of shaking in them. He wished he hadn't blurted out those words. He looked back at Jenny, and her face was white. He gave her a twisted grin.

Cabe's voice seemed to come alive. "I'll get the boys. They're in the bunkhouse. It's going to take all of us to get a saddle on him."

An understanding grew in Vaughan's eyes. "You worked for this, didn't you, Dandy? I won't forget that." He followed Ashel toward the barn.

Jenny remained on the top rail, biting her lower lip.

It took three ropes on Fireball before they could even begin to get near him. The ropes pulled him in three different directions, choking him down. Cabe managed to get a bandanna tied around the animal's eyes, and the stallion quieted. A man had to watch every movement he made around the horse. Fireball. The horse could use teeth or hoofs with equal dexterity. Ashel wouldn't let anyone else saddle him. He threw the saddle across Fireball's back and saw the quiver ran the length of the barrel. He tested the cinch strap and was satisfied it was drawn up to the last hole. He gathered the reins in his hand, put his boot in the stirrup, and threw his weight onto his left leg. Fireball crouched, but that was all. Ashel read the warning in that crouching. The stallion was wasting no time in futile effort. His time was coming.

Ashel swung into the saddle and looked about him. Vaughan sat beside Jenny, and their faces were tight. Cabe and Lanny and Pete had their ropes on Fireball. Tom sat his horse just outside the gate. Their faces were shining with eager expectation. Ashel hoped all of them stayed in their saddles. If anything went wrong, he wanted them to come after him as fast as they could.

He gingerly loosened one rope and cast it off. Lanny pulled slowly out of the corral. Ashel threw the second loop to the ground. Fireball's hide twitched whenever Ashel touched it. He cast off Cabe's loop, and he was alone in the corral. The stallion seemed poised on great steel springs, contracted springs waiting for the right moment to unloosen and throw Ashel into the sky.

He loosened the bandanna and threw it from him. At the top of his lungs he yelled, "Hiyah."

Fireball didn't go into immediate action. This was an old story to him, and it almost looked as though some evil intelligence was measuring the situation. He left the ground as though he were trying to fly. The move came with vicious suddenness, and if a rider were not alert, that first jump would have unseated him. The animal came down on stiffened legs, squalling with primitive fury. Ashel's chin lashed backward under the force of the impact, and his neck took punishment. He'd never known a horse to go as high, or to land as hard. He had little time to think about it, for the bucking plunges came too rapidly. The earth was a great rubber ball, bouncing Fireball from it every time his hoofs touched it. The horse had a trick of putting most of its weight on it hindquarters, then springing straight upward, reversing itself as it came down, landing on stiffened forelegs. Each landing was like being hit with a club at the base of the spine. Ashel didn't know how many springs like that the stallion made. They came in such rapid succession that there was hardly a breath between. His neck was a piece of string, and his head lolled helplessly about on it. His world was a spinning blur, tilting first one way, then the other. The hammering his spine took transmitted sickness to his stomach, and he felt the queasy hollow spread. The last lunge had as much vigor in it as the first. This horse wasn't made of flesh. It was made of iron.

Ashel's breath tightened into a knot in his throat as Fireball sprang upward again. The jarring landing sent his breath free in a rushing gush, and its force seemed to tear the tissues of his throat.

Fireball varied his tactics. He landed on one stiffened foreleg, and that sent a different jolting through Ashel. He lit on both forelegs, sending solid rolls of shock through his rider. Then he bowed his back and lit on all fours, and that was the worst of all.

Ashel was a mass of hurt inside, and something warm and sticky filled his mouth. The hammering made him gasp for breath, and a dismal thought was filtering into his mind. I can't stick on him.

Fireball wasted no energy in trying to cover distance. He went up and came down in a tiny area, each hoof seeming to land in the print of the last. If anything, he seemed to be gaining strength.

Dust from the pounding hoofs engulfed Ashel. His muscles were beginning to go flaccid, and he knew the next plunge would unseat him. He survived that one, then another. The third one twisted him in the saddle, and he lost balance. Fireball gave him no time to recover. He spun in a tight circle, and the force pulled Ashel's upper body lower and lower toward the ground. He made his decision. He could stay until the last plunge, be thrown, and risk trampling under savage hoofs, before anyone could get to him. Or he could jump from the saddle and run for the corral walls.

He kicked one boot free and swung his leg over the pommel. He jerked the other foot out of the stirrup, and as he made his jump from the saddle, Fireball twisted in the opposite direction, throwing Ashel off balance. He came down heavily on one foot, felt it twist beneath him, and started a limping run toward the bars. He heard a furious squalling, and above it, the higher notes of a woman's scream. He dared not look behind him. He took a few more strides, and a brutal force smashed into his back. He tried to ball and roll as he went down, but his head struck the earth, and a great, black blanket instantly blotted out the light.

CHAPTER TWELVE

He didn't want to open his eyes. The darkness was a form of security. The light would bring waves of pain. He gingerly lifted an arm and was surprised it would respond. At least Fireball had not stomped him there. He opened his eyes, and for a moment could not realize where he was. He should be lying in the corral dust, but he was in bed. The time of day was wrong, too, for the sun was streaming through the east window. The last he remembered, it had been almost sundown.

They must have carried him into the house, and it was morning. He thought, hell, I wasn't out the whole night, was I? He sat up, and a grunt escaped him. His upper body felt as though it was one solid bruise. He remembered there had been a stabbing pain in his ankle as he landed, and he threw the light covering from him. The ankle was swollen, and its color was something to see. Black and deep purple, blended with yellow. He didn't have to test that ankle to know he wouldn't walk on it for a while.

Someone had undressed him when they put him in bed, and his face burned. He hoped it wasn't Millie or Jenny.

He lifted his voice in a tentative "Hello," then strengthened it the second time. He heard footsteps outside the door, lay back, and drew the covering over him.

Millie came into the room, and Jenny followed her. Millie carried a tray, and Ashel's stomach rumbled at the good smells coming from it.

Millie asked coldly, "Do you feel like eating now?"

"Are you mad at me?" he asked.

Her frown increased. "I'm mad at you." She could keep up the pretense no longer, and she cried, "Ashel, do you know you could've been killed?"

"It ran through my mind," he confessed. "Particularly when I felt Fireball's breath on my neck. Is Milo mad at me too?"

"He's mad," Millie said.

Jenny's eyes were shining. "And proud too. Do you know you rode Fireball longer than anybody else has? Didn't you hear them yelling for you? They thought you were going to make it. They're still talking about it this morning."

"What happened out there?" he asked.

"Don't you remember Fireball smashing into you?"

He nodded. He remembered that. "I felt him hit me. After that, everything was black."

Jenny said, "Tom got through the gate just before you jumped. He hazed Fireball from you. You should've heard Milo cussing and yelling orders. He and Tom carried you into the house and put you in bed."

That was good. Millie or Jennie hadn't had a hand in that.

Millie said fiercely, "You frightened us to death last night. We tried to talk to you, and you mumbled a few words and went back to sleep."

He shook his head. He didn't remember that at all. He guessed he owed a lot to Tom. Fireball would have trampled the life out of him as he lay unconscious.

"What made you do it?" Millie asked. "Didn't they tell you Fireball was a killer?"

"They told me. But Dandy seemed to be egging me on. I wanted to try it."

Millie's voice was tart. "If it's any satisfaction to you, you rode him longer than Dandy could. What good does it do you?"

He looked at Jenny. He imagined her eyes held a new respect. He thought the effort did him a lot of good.

Millie's voice remained tart. "I suppose you want to try it again?"

She was asking him that, and he wasn't over the first attempt. "No," he said honestly. "I've had enough."

Millie set the tray down beside him. "Maybe all the sense wasn't knocked out of your head. Jenny, feed him. I've got other things to do."

"Aw, now," he protested. "I can feed myself."

"You'll take orders," Millie said and left the room.

Jenny's eyes danced as she cut a bite of steak. She extended the fork toward him. "You heard Millie."

His face was flaming as he took the bite. "I'm no baby." The words lacked conviction. What man wouldn't enjoy a girl as pretty as this feeding him?

He ate a big breakfast of steak and eggs and fried pota-toes. When he tried to talk between bites, she shook her head at him.

He finished the last bite, and she said, "At least, you didn't hurt your appetite. We'll bandage your ankle, when we're sure the swelling's stopped."

He stuck his foot from under the cover and looked at the

ankle. "It's not bad. I'll be walking tonight."

"You will not," she said sharply. She picked up the tray and started toward the door.

"You're coming back?" he asked.

She smiled at him. "I'm coming back."

He sighed with contentment as the door closed. An excitement was spreading through him. She cared for him. He wasn't foolish in thinking that. She showed it in a dozen ways—her concern for him, and her attempts at making him more comfortable—they were just two of the ways. The marvel of it grew, making his breathing ragged. He guessed love could hit a man and woman this fast.

She came back into the room and asked, "Why don't you try to go back to sleep?"

Sleep was the last thing he wanted. He shook his head.

"Do you want me to read to you?"

He considered that. While she read, he could watch her. He shook his head again. "I'd rather talk."

She moved to the bed. "Let me fluff up your pillow."

He lifted his head, and she withdrew the pillow. As she pounded it back into shape, she was close to him. She had a good, clean smell, a woman's smell.

He said huskily, "Jenny."

"Yes." She turned her face to him.

Those slightly parted, full lips were invitation. He slid his arm about her shoulder, pulled her nearer, and attempted to kiss her.

She jerked her head to one side, and his lips brushed her cheek.

"Don't. Please." She pulled away and straightened. Distress was in her eyes.

He said hoarsely, "Jenny," and held out his hands to her. "Don't you know I—"

"Don't say it," she interrupted. "Ashel, I'm to be married within two weeks. My fiancé is coming from the East, and we're to be married here. Didn't Millie tell you?"

Being hit with a club couldn't have stunned him more. It erased the words from his tongue, the thoughts from his head. He groped in a void, trying to find something to hold on to. Bitterness crept in, filling that void. She could have told him, she could have stopped him making a fool of himself.

"Ashel," she said. "I'm sorry." She wanted to say more, and she, too, had trouble in finding words.

Sanity replaced some of the bitterness, and he stared soberly at her. She had offered him kindness and friendship, and he had taken it for something else. It wasn't her fault. It wasn't really anybody's fault.

He hurt pretty bad inside, and he guessed that would go on for a while. But she couldn't be blamed for that. He said, "Jenny, a man isn't acting natural unless he's making a fool of himself. Will you forgive me?"

She blinked hard, and tears came into her eyes. "There's nothing to forgive. No woman can be offended, when she's been paid a compliment."

He said "Thanks," and stared at the ceiling. "Does Dandy know?"

Her eyes were startled. "I haven't told him. Why should he know?"

"He's in love with you, Jenny."

She gasped and said, "That's ridiculous, Ashel. He's almost as old as Milo." Her cheeks flamed, and her eyes would not quite meet his.

"He is," Ashel insisted. "I've watched him. I think you know it, too. That's why you've been avoiding him."

Her eyes grew troubled. "Ashel, I don't want to hurt him. I talked to Millie and Milo. We decided not to announce it until the last minute."

"You're going to hurt him," he said bluntly. "It might be wisest to tell him now. To give him time to recover." She could tell him to shut his mouth, to stay out of something that was none of his business. But she should know Dandy's nature. He might go wild when he heard about this.

She gnawed her lower lip. Her voice was weak. "I've got to think about it, Ashel. Will you call me, if you need anything?"

"Sure," he said. "And I'll ask you the same thing."

Her smile was shaky, but it was there. "Agreed," she said and moved out of the room.

He stared at the closed door. He felt empty inside. He could be her friend and no more. He thought morosely, *After she's married, I'll never see her again.* It was best that way, and it was no help at all. He sank lower and lower in the bog of his miserable thoughts.

It must have showed in his face when Vaughan came into the room an hour later. "You look like somebody stepped on your tail," Vaughan said. He squinted at Ashel. "And Jenny's moping around outside. Say! Did you two have a quarrel."

"No quarrel, Milo." He wanted to get Vaughan off the subject before the man saw how lacerated his feelings were. He said, "I've been lying here doing some thinking,

Milo. Will the homesteaders and cattlemen ever learn to live together?"

"Not on any common ground." Vaughan said it harshly.

"Do you hate them that bad?"

Vaughan shook his head. "I don't hate them at all. If I feel anything for them, it's pity. They're bucking something they can't beat. The worst of it is they won't only hurt themselves. They'll hurt everyone around them."

"How?" Ashel couldn't keep the challenge out of his voice.

Vaughan sat down beside the bed. "Did you ever hear of John Powell?" He grinned as Ashel shook his head. "You were pretty small when Powell was out here. He was a director or something in the United States Geological Survey. We called him the preacher. He was the first man to ever preach water conservation around here. I saw the report he made in 1878. He claimed Montana never could be cropped because of limited rain and recurrent drought. According to him, successful cropping takes about twenty inches of rain a year, and that kind of fall stops about fifty miles east of Pembina, North Dakota. Some years we go as low as five inches. Plowing causes gullying, sheet erosion, and alkalization of the ground. I'll bet I've seen ten thousand acres ruined because it was plowed. After the sod is turned, runoff water cuts gullies in the earth and the alkali comes up."

Ashel listened intently. Vaughan sounded as though he had made an intensive study of weather and soil conditions here. He thought of his family and of their struggle against the stubborn land. "You don't think any homesteader has a chance?"

"None. Unless they live on a stream and can irrigate. The homesteaders aren't the only guilty ones. Back in the eighties, the cattlemen hurt the land as much as any sod-buster. Powell also warned against overgrazing. It takes too long for the grass to come back. If cattle eat the grass down too far, they can kill the sod. That's as bad as plowing. It takes a man a long time to learn anything. And he won't profit by the experience of others. He's got to learn it himself. The hard way. I saw an old Indian watching a home-steader plow. It was plowing pretty good, turning the sod under and bringing up moisture. That old Indian squatted and ran his hand into the fresh dirt. He looked at the home-steader and grunted, 'Wrong side up.'"

Vaughan grinned at his recollection. "It was kind of funny but a sad funny. That old Indian knew. The sod held what little moisture there was in the ground. The plow turned it up so that the sun could get at it. The homesteader cussed the Indian for an ignorant savage. Three years later, the homesteader was gone. I rode by that place the other day. The grass still hasn't come back."

He pointed his finger at Ashel. "It makes you kind of sick to see these people come out all filled up with hope. And they haven't got a chance. You try to tell them what they're up against, and they shout that you don't want them here. By God, I don't. Not under these conditions. Powell said a quarter-section is not enough to support one family. He fixed four square miles as the absolute minimum, and what does the government offer the homesteader?" Vaughan snorted. "A hundred and sixty acres."

"I thought you said Powell worked for the government."

Vaughan nodded. "He did. Did you ever hear of the government listening to anyone? Even their own people?"

Vaughan stared across the room, and his thoughts were far in the past. "I said cattlemen hurt this country. We damned near made a desert out of it. Other people helped. Like General James S. Brisbin. You ever hear of him?"

Ashel shook his head and grunted as he shifted his weight. He looked at his ankle and said, "It's sore."

"I imagine. Feel like going to sleep?"

Ashel shook his head. He wanted to hear Vaughan talk. It was hard not to believe a man when he quoted facts and figures.

"Who was Brisbin?"

"He wrote a book." Vaughan looked as though he tasted something sour. "*The Beef Bonanza*, or *How to Get Rich on the Plains*. It came out in '81 or '82. I read it. Biggest bunch of horse shit a man ever waded through. Brisbin said all the flocks and herds in the world could find ample grass in Montana. He had figures to show a $100,000 investment could be doubled easily in five years and pay an annual dividend of ten per cent. He had a letter in that book he claimed was from a rancher to his brother. That rancher put in $3,060 and it grew to $100,000. All he had to put out at the start was a hundred dollars for a Studebaker wagon, a hundred and fifty dollars for two yoke of oxen, and ten dollars a month to an Indian herder. The grass was all free."

Ashel laughed at the expression on Vaughan's face.

"It's kind of funny now," Vaughan admitted. "It wasn't then. People believed stuff like that. Big cattle companies were formed, and they pushed thousands of heads onto the range. We even had a French nobleman who came over to get in on the easy money. We had a couple of warnings during the early eighties. A couple of bad winters, but we pulled through and nobody paid any attention. A ten per cent loss of herd in winter is normal. A summer drought makes the losses worse. You get a shortage of feed and cattle go into winter poor. During a drought cattle will eat poisonous weeds, which they wouldn't ordinarily touch. And drought always brings a fire or two."

Vaughan rolled a cigarette, his fingers working slowly. He wasn't merely talking; he was reliving bad experiences.

He said, "Nothing is as bad as prairie fire. Nothing can live after it. Gophers come up from their holes and starve to death in the ashes. So does everything else. A fire will sweep at forty or fifty miles an hour, faster than a horse can run. After a fire the herd has to be moved to new grazing grounds. They can't live on the old range until the new grass comes next spring. Then it lacks nourishment because the moisture-holding mulch is gone, and the grass isn't as hardy. I've made two drives like that. Forced drives. You push the cattle as hard as you can. They shuffle through miles of ashes, their hoofs throwing up clouds of sooty, weightless dust. Cattle and men turn black. Your face cracks and your eyes burn, and there's nothing but that damned blackness wherever you look. It doesn't take cattle long to go crazy with thirst. If they stampede, they have to be headed in the direction of water and grass, for every mile they cover is taking a toll. A few miles in the wrong direction could be your margin." Vaughan shook his head. "I never want to see another prairie fire."

"Can you stop one?" Ashel asked.

"If you catch it early enough and move fast. The best way is to shoot a steer and drag the carcass with a rope.

That will smother a small fire." Vaughan grinned at the expression on Ashel's face. "Shooting a fifty-dollar steer sounds expensive, doesn't it? I'd shoot a couple dozen to stop a fire.

"The summer of 1886 burned us up," he went on. "Cattle prices were going to hell. That year we got less than four dollars a hundred at Chicago with a freight bill of six dollars a head. And more cattle were being pushed into Montana. The grass started dying in July, and it took a big stream or waterhole to keep from going dry. That fall we saw animals that ordinarily winter here moving south. Horses and cattle started growing heavier, shaggier coats of hairs. *Kissin-ey-oo-way'-o,* the Crees said. It blows cold. They sure as hell were right. The first cold hit us in November. We don't expect any really bad weather until after Christmas. That wind was full of pieces of ice. It started out by roaring, then picked up to a moaning and screaming. Snow rode the wind, slashing like a million knives. It kept piling higher and higher, and when a horse or cow stumbled into a drift, the meat on their legs was cut to the bone. I never saw the white owls before. The Indians said they came from the Arctic, that they were flying south to get out of the worst of it. Worst of it?" Vaughan's grin was bleak. "They landed right in the middle of it.

"In December we got two more blizzards. The Indians call January the Moon of Cold-exploding Trees. On the ninth it snowed for sixteen straight hours, an inch an hour. The temperature went to twenty-two below zero, and we got more snow for the next ten days. The temperature got lower and lower. On the twenty-eighth, the big blizzard hit. For three days and nights you couldn't see fifty feet in any direction. The temperature dropped to sixty-three below. When a man got off his horse, he dropped into snow waist deep on level ground. The cattle were starving. Their bodies were covered with sores and frozen blood. They drifted before the wind, piling up against barb-wire fences. They died there. I've seen them trapped in drifts above their bellies, held up until they froze. I don't know how many slid into air holes in the rivers and drowned."

Ashel shivered. Vaughan made it very real. Ashel thought of people he knew—of Millie and Tom and Lanny going through something like that. Jenny wasn't too old then, but she would have been touched by it, too. The increasing strain in her parents' faces would have strung her tight.

"What could you do?" he asked.

"Not very much. We put on two suits of heavy under-wear, two pairs of wool socks, wool pants, two woolen shirts, overalls and leather chaps. We wore wool gloves under leather mittens and blanket-lined overcoats and fur caps. Before putting on the socks we walked barefoot in the snow, then rubbed our feet dry. After we put on boots we stood in water, then went outdoors until an air-tight sheath of ice formed on the boots. It helped for a while. We blacked our faces and eye sockets with burnt matches or cut eye holes in black neckerchiefs to keep from going snow blind. We looked like a bunch of bandits. We couldn't do much. We pulled a few cows out of drifts and tried to herd them into sheltered ravines. We tried to keep them away from the rivers. That cold ate out your lungs. You could feel it clear down into your belly. Frozen hands and feet were pretty common. Two of my men died. All we could do was to shove them into a snowbank until a Chinook came and thawed the ground enough to dig a grave."

Ashel saw Vaughan's hands fisted in his lap. A man never forgot an experience like that. The wonder of it was that he could keep on.

"The storms and cold lasted through February," Vaughan said. "Every town had its streets filled with starving cattle. They ate the bushes and saplings down to the ground. They ate garbage, anything they could find. And they died in the yards of those towns. The Chinook came in March, a month later than usual. We learned how bad it was during the May roundup. But most of us already knew. I've seen coulees and sheltered valleys a man couldn't ride into because of the smell from rotting carcasses. We had a sixty per cent loss for the state. Over three hundred thousand head. I lost eighteen hundred out of three thousand head. We were broke but good. Everyone rushed cattle to the market trying to get a few dollars. And the price dropped to twenty-six dollars for a twelve-hundred-pound steer. It cost twenty dollars a head to restock, and a lot of us couldn't afford it. That French marquis gave up and went off to India to shoot tigers. The Swan Cattle Company, backed by Scotch money, went under. The Niobrara Cattle Company had nine thousand head left out of thirty-nine thousand. It broke them. It took the ones who stayed several years to even begin to beat back. But we learned something. I know I'll never own another animal I can't feed and shelter." He stood and look at Ashel. "That's why I'm against the sodbuster. Maybe not so much them as what they're doing. You abuse this land, and it's going to hit back. And it can hit a hell of a lot harder than you think."

Ashel had heard some of the homesteaders complain about the amount of land that cattlemen like Vaughan owned. He thought, they've earned that land. Every foot of it.

Vaughan said, "I imagine supper's about ready." He looked squarely at Ashel. "I guess you've wondered about Dandy, about the leeway I give him. Dandy went through all that with me. Every step of the way."

Ashel saw Dandy Cabe in a new light. And he learned a new respect for the man. He said, "Milo, you'll never have any trouble from me about Dandy. I'll do my best to stay out of his way."

Vaughan's smile was warm. "I kinda thought it'd be that way. If I can find a crutch, you feel like limping in to supper?"

"Sure," Ashel said. He would work a little harder trying to make Dandy accept him.

CHAPTER THIRTEEN

In a week, Ashel was limping about without the aid of a crutch. He kept away from the house as much as possible. It still hurt whenever he looked at Jenny. He had nothing to offer this girl, and he knew it. It had been a fool's dream, but still it had its glitter. A man locked up those kinds of dreams—forever.

He was replacing a board Blackie had kicked loose in his stall, when he heard voices outside. That was Cabe and Jenny talking, and Ashel straightened. He didn't want to overhear, but there was no way he could avoid it.

"Will you quit following me around, Dandy?" Jenny

sounded exasperated.

"Are you trying to avoid me, Jenny?" Cabe asked in a frozen voice.

"No," Jenny said weakly. "But every time I turn a corner, you pop out at me. Haven't you got work to do?"

The cold quality remained in Cabe's voice. "I get my complaints from Milo. Not you."

Ashel could imagine how Jenny looked. She had Millie's fire. She said, "Then just let me alone. That's all I'm asking."

The silence was prolonged, and Ashel thought, Cabe must be staring at her.

Then Cabe said, "I'll do the deciding about that, too."

Ashel heard the faint beat of his footsteps, then the sound faded.

Jenny came into the barn. "Ashel," she called.

He stepped out of the stall. "How did you know I was here?" he asked gruffly.

"I saw you come in. Have you been avoiding me?"

He tried to make a joke of it. "Seems like everybody's asking that."

He saw the stillness settle over her face. "I couldn't help but hear, Jenny."

"I'm not blaming you." Her voice was low. "I've never seen him like he was just now. He looked mean. If he keeps on bothering me, I'm going to tell Milo."

Ashel's face was sober. This was the side of Dandy Cabe she had probably never seen. What would Milo do if Jenny went to him? Make excuses for Cabe or straighten him out? Vaughan would be torn in two directions.

He asked, "Have you told Dandy yet?"

She would not meet his eyes. "I've tried. The time never seemed quite right." She saw the accusation in his eyes. "I'm going to tell him, Ashel."

He wanted to tell her how foolish she was in putting it off, but he kept silent. It was Jenny's business, and she would have to handle it the way she saw fit.

He looked anxiously at the door. He didn't want Cabe coming in and finding them together. He said, "Jenny, it won't help Dandy's temper any if he finds you talking to me."

His words struck spark from her. "I will not be governed by what Dandy Cabe thinks I should do."

He wasn't quite that free. Not as long as he worked here. He said, "Besides I've got work to do." His smile took the sting out of the excuse.

Some of her temper turned on him. "You have not. I heard Milo tell you he didn't want you working until that ankle was fully healed. I'll talk to you whenever I want to. And you, or Dandy, or anyone else can't tell me not to."

She stalked out of the barn, her strides as long as a man's. She would do as she said. She had a lot of Vaughan's stubbornness in her.

If she did as she said, it meant trouble with Cabe. Ashel had no doubt of that. He might not be able to handle the next trouble with Cabe. He could quit, or he could ask Vaughan for a different job, one that kept him away from the house most of the time.

He caught Vaughan after supper that night and said, "Milo, I'm pretty well caught up with mending things around here."

Vaughan's eyes were serious. "You trying to say you're

quitting, Ashel?"

Ashel shook his head. "I want something different to do. After listening to you the other night, I want to learn something about cattle. I can't do it sawing and hammering boards."

"Well, now." Vaughan s eyes shone with pleasure. "We'll talk about it when you get around better."

"I want to start in the morning. I can mend fence. Wouldn't that save you some man hours? I could report on grass and water. I know what to look for."

Vaughan nodded. "It'd be a help. Nobody's looked much after fence for over a year. That ankle wouldn't stop you from riding. You can start in the morning."

Ashel said, "Thanks, Milo."

Vaughan looked surprised, and Ashel did not stop to explain.

He walked into the bunkhouse, and Cabe sat on the edge of his bunk. His eyes had a hard shine.

They were alone, and the troubled thought swept through Ashel's mind. If he crowds me, will Vaughan believe me when I tell him I wanted no part of it?

Cabe pointed a finger at him. "Because I haven't been paying any attention to you, Honyocker, don't think I've forgotten anything."

"Dandy, I don't want any more trouble. All I want is to do my job and—"

Cabe swore at him. "You turned Millie against me. Now you're trying to turn Jenny." He stood and took a couple of steps toward Ashel.

Ashel thought, I can't help it, Milo, but here goes my promise to you. He would not run. Not even to keep out of trouble with Cabe.

Cabe's eyes were wicked coals. "I saw Jenny come out of the barn this morning. She wouldn't speak to me. What did you tell her?"

Ashel sighed. He was afraid Cabe had seen them. "Nothing, Dandy. We were just talking about my work."

"You goddamned liar," Cabe roared. Before he could move, Tom came into the room.

Tom put an interested appraisal on them and asked, "You two arguing again?"

Cabe whirled on him, his face livid. "I'm not forgetting you, either. The first man we don't need around here is you." He stomped out of the bunkhouse and slammed the door.

"What's eating him?" Tom asked in astonishment.

Ashel shook his head. Cabe had a big hatred. It reached out and included anyone who was friendly to Ashel. "You know Dandy."

"I know he's getting damned hard to live with," Tom growled.

He hadn't asked Vaughan to give him a new job any too soon, Ashel thought. He had to stay out of Cabe's way until after Jenny was married. Cabe would see then how wrong his jealousy of Ashel was.

He saddled Blackie in the morning. He filled a saddlebag with staples and picked up hammer and pliers. Vaughan came to the barn and said, "Take a gun with you."

A tight knot formed in Ashel's throat. Had it gone so far that Vaughan thought he needed a gun to protect himself?

Vaughan said, "A rider never knows when he'll need one.

You might need it to kill a snake or a wolf. You might see a steer with a busted leg." He handed Ashel a pistol.

Ashel shook his head. "I never handled one. I couldn't hit the barn with it. I will take a rifle." He could handle a rifle. He had sharpened his eye on squirrels in the Missouri Ozarks.

Vaughan nodded. "I'll get one out of the house."

He came back with a rifle and a coiled rope. He handed Ashel the carbine. Ashel pulled it out of its boot and examined it. It was a sweet little gun.

"That will stop any lobo," Vaughan said. He hung the coiled rope over the horn.

"Milo, I can't use that. I never threw a rope in my life."

Vaughan frowned at him, but there was amusement in his eyes. "If you're going to be a puncher, you've got to look like one. You might need it, Ashel. It won't hurt to take it along. You could find an animal bogged down. I've seen them pinned under a deadfall. A man with a rope can jerk them free. You can walk up to a trapped animal and place a loop around its neck, can't you? Blackie will do the rest."

Ashel mounted and put Blackie in motion. He looked back, and Vaughan was watching him. He wondered if Vaughan was kidding him.

Cabe and the others had already ridden out, and Ashel picked the opposite direction. He rode along the fence, checking each post for missing staples. At times he could ride past a dozen posts before he dismounted, hobbled to the fence, and hammered in a missing staple. Weather was always working on a fence post, checking and cracking it. When the crack opened up enough and a staple was in line with it, the staple fell out. It was going to take a long time to ride all the fence Vaughan owned. He shouldn't be through before Jenny was gone.

He topped a small rise and halted Blackie. He loosened the reins and let the horse graze. There was good grass here, but it was beginning to brown. It would green up with the first rain, but this could be another drought year, followed by a winter like the one Vaughan described. He looked out over the sweep of country and drew a deep breath. Could he go through such a winter? He felt the challenge the question posed. A man could have a quiet pride if he ever fought weather like that.

He turned in the saddle, his eyes covering more country. He stiffened as he saw two men not over five hundred yards away. Their horses were behind them, and for a moment he took the two to be part of Cabe's crew. The men were hunkered down, and from this distance he couldn't tell what they were doing.

Quite a distance behind the men, cattle grazed. The two men could be working over a downed animal, maybe a calf, too small to be seen from this distance.

As Ashel watched he saw a red eye of flame wink into existence and strengthen. A brisk breeze was blowing from the two men toward the cattle. A second red eye appeared and grew.

The realization of what they were doing hit Ashel hard. They were firing the grass. The breeze joined the two red eyes into a short line of fire, and the two men moved to a new position and stooped over.

Vaughan's words about prairie fires rang in Ashel's head. Why, goddamn them, he thought furiously. The thought shook him out of his shock. He jerked the carbine from its scabbard and yelled, "Hiyah."

He jerked Blackie's head up and spurred him into a run. His yell or the pound of Blackie's hoofs carried to the men, for he saw them straighten and look toward him. He fired a shot over their heads, and they broke into a run for their horses. Ashel demanded more speed from Blackie. He had never known such a murderous rage. He would put the next two shots through their black, destroying hearts.

He cut the distance in half before he recognized the two horses. That brought a different kind of shock. Those two horses were Lady and Nellie. The two men had to be Hobe and Nobby.

Hobe and Nobby reached their animals and attempted to mount. The horses were spooked, and they skittered around, making it difficult for Hobe and Nobby to control them. They finally mounted and galloped off at a heavy, awkward pace.

Ashel was close enough to pick either off his mount's back. The carbine butt was against his shoulder, then he lowered it. He couldn't shoot his brothers. But he could run them down and beat hell out of them.

The fire! While he was running Hobe and Nobby down, the fire would gain a terrible advantage. He looked at it, and the line had lengthened and strengthened. He even thought he could hear its crackling.

He let Hobe and Nobby go and spun Blackie. He sobbed deep in his throat as near panic seized him. The god-damned wind. With it pushing the fire, one man could never stomp it out.

Drag a carcass across it. The words popped into his head as though Vaughan were saying them now. He turned

Blackie and raced toward the grazing cattle. They threw up their heads at his approach and stood in indecision. In a moment, they would break and scatter in all directions.

He picked one of the smaller animals, afraid that Blackie could not drag a bigger one fast enough. He made a good shot. He dropped the animal, then fired again as it attempted to rise. Ashel threw off and ran toward it, forgetting the sensitive ankle. The rest of the cattle were in full flight, running with the wind, and Ashel remembered what Vaughan said about the speed of a fire. If this fire was not stopped, it would run over those cattle. He had killed a half-grown calf, and he judged it to weigh somewhere around four hundred pounds. Blackie should be able to drag it.

He looked back at the fire, and it was frightening to see how it had grown. The line of it had tripled in length, and it was creating its own draft speeding its forward progress.

He had forgotten to bring the rope, and he swore at himself. He ran back to Blackie, led him nearer the dead calf, and shook out a loop. He placed it over the calf's head and tied the other end about the horn. He mounted and turned Blackie, and the rope tightened outside his leg.

Blackie was unhappy about the strange weight bouncing and flopping behind him, and Ashel quirted him to get him moving. Between spurs and quirt, he forced him into a full run. He kept pressure on the horse, not giving him time to consider what he was pulling. He aimed toward the near end of the fire, and now Blackie had something else to fear—the leaping, swirling fire ahead of him. He slowed despite the sting of spurs and whip, and Ashel redoubled his efforts, lashing the horse on alternate sides. He kept yelling, "Hiyah, hiyah," in a loud, savage voice, and the combination of punishment and sound forced Blackie on.

The calf bounced and tumbled along the ground, and when its body passed over the line of fire, the fire was blotted out. Ashel kept Blackie just inside the stretch of fire, and the breeze blew tongues of flame at them. He could feel the heat through the sole of his right boot, and he was certain he could smell singed hair on Blackie. The smoke swirled and twisted about him, and he coughed as the acrid fumes bit into his lungs. He kept up that merciless punishment of Blackie, never letting him swerve or hesitate.

It seemed as though he rode through fire and smoke for an eternity, then suddenly the smoke was gone, and he was out into clear, fresh air. His lungs ached, and his heart pounded at a fearful rate, and he heard Blackie's labored breathing.

He pulled the horse to a stop and let him stand on wide-braced legs, head hanging between them. Sweat stood out in dark patches on Blackie's shoulders and flanks, and gouts of foam dripped from its muzzle.

He touched the animal's neck, then ran toward the line of fire. Any attention for Blackie would have to wait until he was sure the last spark was out.

The fire had spread with appalling rapidity in just those few seconds, covering a front of more than two hundred yards. He moved along it, stomping every glowing ember he saw. Soot rose and plastered against his sweating face, and additional sweating cut rivulets through the black coating. He stopped and rested when he reached the far end. Here and there a tiny plume of smoke twisted toward the sky, but he was sure the fire was out. Only then did he realize how weary he was. His legs trembled with every step as he moved toward Blackie.

He uncapped the canteen and spit out the first few mouthfuls to rid himself of the ashes. He drank long, then poured the remainder of the canteen into his hat for Blackie. He listened to the animal's noisy, greedy sucking, knowing just how Blackie felt.

When Blackie sucked the last few drops from his hat, Ashel examined its legs. The hair was singed on them, but he found no burned area of hide. Just the same he would rub salve on them tonight.

He loosened the rope from the calf's neck and slowly coiled it as he looked at the animal. Most of the body hide was gone, and the mangled flesh shone through. A few moments ago it was alive and grazing, representing a tangible asset. Now it was nothing.

Ashel looked at the blackened area the fire left. Ten minutes more and he could not have handled it by himself.

He mounted heavily and turned Blackie toward home. The fence riding would have to wait until tomorrow. As he rode he thought of Hobe and Nobby, and his eyes were bleak. He would have to report the fire to Vaughan. How far should he go? Should he name his brothers? Ashel shook his head. Vaughan would be sure to retaliate, and Ashel did not know what form it would take. If it were only Hobe and Nobby, Ashel would let them take whatever was handed to them. But there were his mother and father to consider. He had to protect Hobe and Nobby for his parents' sake. They won't get off with nothing, he thought. I'll make them afraid to even think fire again.

He had gone less than a mile when he saw two horsemen

coming toward them. He pulled up and waited for Vaughan and Cabe.

Vaughan spurred forward, leaving Cabe behind. When Vaughan reached Ashel, he said, "We saw smoke." He looked at Ashel's soot-blackened face. "What happened?"

"I was in a fire," Ashel said wearily. He saw the strain seize Vaughan's face. "I got it out, Milo."

Cabe came up in time to hear Ashel's words. "It couldn't have been a very big fire," he growled.

Ashel nodded. "It wasn't. I got it right after it started."

"Are you sure it's out?" Anxiety was in Vaughan's voice. "I want to check it."

"It's out, Milo." Ashel could understand Vaughan's anxiety, but it meant an additional two-mile ride for him.

He fell in behind Vaughan and Cabe, not forcing Blackie to meet their pace. By the time he arrived at the scene of the fire, they were staring at the blackened area.

Cabe looked at the dead calf, then at Ashel. "Who told you to go around shooting M swinging V stock?"

Protest darkened Ashel's eyes. He was bone-weary, he had stopped a fire, and he was entitled to something more than Cabe yelling at him.

"Don't be a damn fool, Dandy," Vaughan said. His tone was sharp enough to pour blood into Cabe's face. "I told him a man might be able to put out a prairie fire by dragging a steer along its line. I'd have spent a dozen steers to stop this fire. He did one hell of a job."

He looked at Ashel and asked quietly, "How did it start, Ashel?" He glanced at the blackened area. "I'd say you caught it pretty early."

"I did, Milo. I came up over that rise." Ashel slewed in

145

his saddle and pointed. "I saw two men setting it. I was too far away to recognize them." He would tell Vaughan a partial truth but no more.

Cabe caught some flicker of uneasy expression in Ashel's eyes, for he kneed his horse toward him. "You knew them," he accused. "Who are you covering?"

Ashel doggedly shook his head. "I didn't know them. It was either go after them or stop the fire. I thought the fire was more important."

"It was," Vaughan said grimly. "It could've swept this range clear to the mountains. If I knew who the bastards were—"

"Look at him," Cabe yelled. "He knows. It was probably some sodbuster friend. Or maybe even his own family."

It was a random shot, and the twitch in Ashel's face showed that it scored.

"I didn't know them," he repeated. It was hard to return Vaughan's look. He saw the doubt creeping into Vaughan's eyes, and it made him heartsick. He felt as though the earth had opened suddenly into a deep, wide gorge and he and Vaughan stood on opposite sides.

Cabe started to yell again, and Vaughan said, "Drop it, Dandy." He turned his horse and put it into a fast lope.

Cabe looked at Ashel. "I got an idea of who it was," he said softly, "and I'm not dropping it." He turned and followed Vaughan.

Ashel stared after them. When you called a man a friend, it cut like hell to see doubt in his eyes.

CHAPTER FOURTEEN

Vaughan found Ashel after supper, leaning against the bunkhouse wall and staring into space. For a moment Vaughan did not say anything. The calculation in his eyes didn't make it a friendly silence.

He rolled a cigarette before he spoke. "Ashel, if that fire had gotten out of hand, it could've put me in a bad bind."

Ashel knew it. He said, "Yes," in a flat voice.

"I'm grateful for your part in it. But if you know those men, I want their names. I want to be damned sure they never try a stunt like that again. Did you know them, Ashel?"

"I didn't know them, Milo." It was hard to force the lie past the constriction in his throat. He was a poor liar. He was sure the evidence rode in his face and voice.

Vaughan thought so, too, for his face went wooden. "All right, Ashel," he said curtly. He turned and moved away, the length and rapidity of his stride showing the anger within him.

Ashel stared mournfully after him. He wished he could tell Vaughan he needn't worry, that the two men would never try to set another fire. Not after he got through talking to them.

He picked up his saddle and moved toward the corral. He hated to put Blackie back to work, but it had to be done.

Cabe and Lanny came out of the barn. Cabe's eyes were narrowed as he watched Ashel's diminishing figure. "Follow him, Lanny, and see where he goes." A small, mean grin parted his lips. "You know, I think we'll be able to run the Honyocker off here after all."

The family sat around the table. All except Elodia. Ashel ordered her outside.

"It wasn't us," Hobe said sullenly for the half-dozenth time.

"You're a liar," Ashel said furiously. "I saw you. If Cabe or the others found you, they'd have put a bullet through you."

His mother gasped, and Paw's mouth worked. They believed Ashel.

"Hobe. Nobby," Paw cried. "Why'd you do it? What did you figure it was going to gain us?"

Neither would look at Paw or Ashel. Nobby's fist was a hard rock on the table. The knuckles stood out in white relief in the lamplight. "It ain't right for one man to have so much. When we got so little. By God, it ain't fair at all."

Ashel stared at them, getting a clear picture of his brothers. They set the fire out of pure envy of another man's holdings. The years of work and hardship meant nothing to them. If he told them about Vaughan's struggle, they wouldn't even try to understand it. They were shiftless and lazy. They would whine about another man's standing and do nothing to improve their own. They would hurt that other man out of spite, just as they had tried to hurt Vaughan.

He remembered the expression on Cabe's face. "I think Cabe knows," he said. "Maybe Milo does, too."

Nobby swung a frightened face toward him. "If they do, you told them."

148

"I should've told them," Ashel said savagely. He felt an inward sickness. He had dimmed the friendship between Vaughan and himself to protect something like this. "If you're ever caught on Milo's land again, they'll shoot you on sight. I'll do it, myself."

"Ashel," Maw cried in horror. "What a terrible thing to say."

"He's turned against us," Paw wailed. "He's one of them now."

"Did you hear me?" Ashel demanded.

His brothers looked at him, and he saw a naked fear in their eyes. They heard him and they believed him. He thought their malice would not touch Milo Vaughan again.

He walked to the door and looked back. The four of them stared at him. The lamplight made their eyes enormous. They looked at him as though he was a stranger.

Lanny said, "He rode straight home, Dandy."

"I thought he would." Cabe's eyes had an ugly shine of triumph. "He'd want to warn his brothers to lay low."

Lanny's expression was doubtful. "But, Dandy, he's been riding over there all the time. How do you know—"

"I know," Cabe said harshly. "They damned near burned us out yesterday. Milo's too chickenhearted to do anything about it. But I will. It's time to run the Honyocker's family out. And the Honyocker with them. They like fire. We'll give it back to them. We'll do a little burning of our own."

Lanny's face lighted. He liked to see the terror on these sodbusters' faces when their barn or house was set on fire. They ran around in circles and squawked like a bunch of chickens at the sight of a hawk.

"When are we going?" he asked.

"In the morning," Cabe replied. It was time to bring it out into the open. He wanted Vaughan to be blamed for it. The homesteaders would rise against Vaughan, but the M swinging V wouldn't stand alone for long. The other cattlemen would come to their aid, and the homesteaders would be driven out en masse. There would be a lot of vacant land in the country, and a man could grab as much of it as he could hold.

"They'll see us in the daylight," Lanny said, his eyes perplexed. Always before, they had worked at night.

"Sure," Cabe said. "It's time to be seen." They would be identified as part of Vaughan's crew, and the word would spread. If this didn't make the sodbusters wild, nothing would.

"Is Pete going with us?"

"We can handle it alone," Cabe said.

It suited Lanny. Something like this broke the monotony of the days. It also got a man out of a day's work. He might pick up something that was worth keeping, though he had never yet seen a Honyocker own anything he wanted. Still a man never knew.

Hobe and Nobby trudged along the dusty road toward town. Hobe kept up a continuous swearing at his father. "God-damn him," he said. "Sending us to town after grub. And not letting us take Nellie and Lady. How's he think we're going to carry it back?"

Nobby's head bobbed in agreement. "He's afraid we'll ride on Vaughan's land. Hell! There's nothing over there I want." He spat into the dust.

"Ashel threw a scare into you last night," Hobe jeered.

Nobby's face crimsoned with anger. "I didn't hear you do any talking back to him. You know he meant what he said. You ain't looking to get shot any more than me." His anger faded, and he said gloomily, "Maybe Paw's right. Maybe we'd better stay out of sight for a while and let them forget about it. You didn't have such a good idea in firing their grass."

Hobe cursed him. He stopped to draw breath and said, "You thought it was a good one yesterday. By God, I'll do it again, whenever I feel like it. None of them scare me."

Nobby caught the bluster in his brother's voice. When Hobe screamed the loudest, he was always trying to cover up something. "You're a damned liar," Nobby said. "You're as scared as I am. Those sons of bitches can get awful mean."

Hobe started to reply, then stopped and stared down the road.

Nobby followed Hobe's gaze. He saw two horsemen just coming out of the bend in the road a half mile ahead of them. By the dust they were raising, they were riding pretty fast.

"Who are they?" he asked.

Hobe shook his head, but a strain was creeping into his face. "I don't know. They ain't running us off the road. We got as much right to it as they have."

Cabe stopped and threw up his hand, and Lanny pulled up beside him. Lanny stared down the road and asked, "Who are they?"

Cabe squinted at the two men on foot. "We might be in

luck, Lanny," he said. "I believe it's the Honyocker's brothers. This will do us just as good as a burning." His expression was wicked. "Ride the bastards down."

He spurred his horse, and Lanny followed him. A rising excitement swept away Lanny's disappointment. This might be as much fun as burning a barn. He had never ridden down a man. He spurred harder, and a series of shrill yips broke from his lips.

Hobe and Nobby pulled to one side of the road. The horsemen were coming at a full run toward them. Hobe said, "They got plenty room to pass. They're going to throw as much dust as they can in our faces."

Nobby's face was tight with apprehension. The horsemen were only fifty yards away before he recognized them. He yelled, "It's Cabe." His voice was a pitch under a scream. He saw the look on Cabe's face, and his voice climbed that pitch. "They're going to ride us down." He broke and ran to his left, heading for the grove of saplings some five hundred yards away. His breathing was a raw sob, tearing his throat lining. He'd never make those trees. A man couldn't outrun a horse.

Hobe heard Nobby, and he saw the intent on Cabe's face. But he couldn't make his muscles respond to the prodding of his fear. He stood in frozen horror until the horse was almost upon him. Then he turned and ran on an angle from Nobby's course. He didn't take a dozen steps before the horse smashed into him. He screamed as he was knocked off his feet and flung to one side. Oh God, the pain. Surely, his back must be broken. He landed hard, and his mouth filled with dust. Now Cabe would wheel his horse and trample him. He tried to rise, and one leg would not respond. Scream after scream tore from his lips as he tried to drag himself along. He looked like a broken-winged bird flopping in the dust.

Lanny had slowed to watch Dandy smash into the man. That sodbuster looked like a bundle of rags flying through the air. Dandy had his man. Now it was time for Lanny to get his. He spun his horse and spurred it. The sodbuster ahead of him kept turning a frightened face over his shoulder. Let him run his heart out, then Lanny would plow on through him. He didn't hear Cabe yelling his name, but he did hear the shots. He wanted to ignore them, but he knew Cabe's temper. He slowed his horse and turned it, his face stamped with resentment. Cabe had his fun, but he didn't want Lanny to have his.

"Let him go, Lanny," Cabe yelled.

Lanny rode up to him, his eyes sullen. He looked back, and the sodbuster was a couple of hundred yards away. "I can still get him, Dandy."

Cabe shook his head, and Lanny exploded. "Goddamn it, Dandy. He'll tell who did this."

Cabe's eyes were bright and hard as he watched Hobe's writhings. "I want him to. Everybody will believe Milo sent us. If this doesn't make those Honyockers come after us, nothing will."

Dandy was probably right, but it didn't take the sullenness from Lanny's face. He looked at the hurt man before he lifted his reins to follow Cabe.

"You hit him real good, Dandy," he said in a grudging tone. He wondered how it would feel to hit a running man with a horse.

CHAPTER FIFTEEN

Vaughan was waiting for Ashel when he came in from his day of fence riding. He said, "Your sister's in the kitchen."

Ashel's face showed alarm. Someone in the family had been hurt or was sick. "What happened?" he asked.

Vaughan shook his head. "She wouldn't tell us anything."

He walked beside Ashel, but Ashel could feel no friendliness in him. Yesterday's fire and its following doubt were still in Vaughan's mind. The strain between them might fade in time. At the moment, Ashel would have bet against it.

He stopped at the kitchen door and looked at his sister. Elodia sat at the kitchen table, staring big-eyed at the piece of cake and glass of milk before her. She wanted it, it showed in her intent stare, but she kept shaking her head at every word Millie said.

Ashel entered the kitchen, and Millie said, "Tell her she can have it, Ashel. I've been trying for a half hour to get her to eat."

Elodia gave a glad cry and jumped to her feet. She ran to her brother and threw her arms about his waist. The intensity of her hug told how relieved she was to see him.

He tousled her hair and said, "It's all right, kid. Millie wants you to have it." He felt a warm wave of affection toward Millie Vaughan.

Elodia shook her head. "No, ma'am. I'm not hungry. Ashel, Paw wants you to come home. Right away." Her face was suddenly frightened, and she wouldn't look at Vaughan.

Strain appeared in Ashel's face. "What is it, Elodia? Is some one hurt?"

"You just come straight home," she said and walked to the door. She looked at Millie. "Thank you, ma'am. And you've got the prettiest, biggest kitchen I ever did see." She turned and bolted out of the door.

Millie's eyes looked suspiciously moist. "She's a sweet little thing."

"I don't know what's happened," Ashel said in a worried voice. "I'll be back as soon as I can, Milo."

Vaughan nodded without speaking, and Millie gave him an odd glance. She moved to the door with Ashel and said, "You let me know if I can do anything."

"I will," Ashel replied and hurried after Elodia.

He gave her a leg-up onto Nellie's broad back and said, "Now what is it?"

She looked at the house and whispered, "Wait until we get down the road. I was scared back there, Ashel."

Ashel said curtly, "Don't be foolish. The Vaughans are the best people in the world."

Her face was solemn. "You won't think so after you hear what I've got to tell you."

He could have shaken her for the mystery she was putting into this. He guessed the only way he could learn what it was all about was to get Blackie and ride a piece with her.

She would not talk until they were out of sight of the Vaughan house. "Hobe's hurt pretty bad. His leg's busted, and the doctor says he's bruised all over. He groans all the time. He must be hurting awful bad."

"Why didn't Nobby or Paw come after me?"

"They're scared to ride on Vaughan's land. Paw didn't think they'd hurt a girl. I was scared though."

"That's damned foolishness," Ashel said impatiently. "Why are they scared to come to Vaughan's house? And how was Hobe hurt?"

"Dandy Cabe rode over him with his horse. Nobby said Dandy knocked Hobe a mile high. I bet it wasn't that much, do you?"

"Nobby's lying. Why would Cabe do it?"

She shook her head. "I don't think he's lying, Ashel. He was so scared his teeth were chattering. He said Milo Vaughan sent Cabe. That Vaughan's going to try to run us off so he can get our land."

"Oh, hell," Ashel said helplessly. He wondered what Hobe and Nobby were up to. Had they cooked up this lie as an additional attempt to embarrass Vaughan? He thought it more than likely, but he couldn't see what it would gain them.

She said wistfully, "Ashel, I sure wanted that piece of cake. I was afraid to touch it. She might've been trying to poison me."

His voice was sharp. "Elodia, the Vaughans are good people. Millie offered you that cake because she wanted you to have it. She and Vaughan wouldn't hurt anyone."

"I dunno." Elodia's headshake was dubious. "You listen to Hobe, and you won't think that way."

Ashel couldn't bear Nellie's slaw pace any longer. He said, "I'm going ahead, Elodia. You're not afraid riding by yourself?"

"Not now. I'm off his damned old land."

He wanted to yell at her, and instead he put spurs to Blackie. He thought savagely as he rode, they even twisted a kid's thinking. But she would see this thing right and change her mind. He would force Hobe and Nobby to admit they were lying.

The room was filled with people when he walked into it. His mother sat in a corner, sobbing softly. From behind the curtains at the end of the room, he heard Hobe's groaning. Elodia was right about this much. Hobe sounded like he hurt like hell.

Paw sat at the table, his thumb rubbing at his beard. Ashel knew that gesture. Paw always did it when he was worried. Clell Reynolds and Suge Thomas sat across from him, and their faces were angry. Nobby squatted on his heels beside Reynolds, his head turned toward the sound of the groans. Elodia was right again. Nobby looked plain scared.

Reynolds looked up at Ashel's entrance. "You got a gall coming here. Or did you mistake this house for Vaughan's?"

Paw cried, "Ashel, Vaughan's trying to run us off. He set Dandy Cabe on Hobe. Nigh killed him, too. They'll wait for us and pick us off one by one." His voice rose higher and higher. "Ashel, what are we going to do?"

Ashel snapped, "You're going to shut up. Until I learn what's happened."

Thomas looked at Reynolds and nodded heavily. "He's turned against his own family, all right. When a son talks to his father like that—"

Ashel whirled on him. "And that goes for you, too.

Clell," he said warningly as Reynolds started to rise, "don't do anything foolish."

He strode to the curtains and parted them. Hobe lay on the bed, his head rolling from side to side. His leg was in splints. "The pain," he kept moaning. "Oh God, the pain."

Ashel's face remained cold. Hobe had a broken leg, but he wasn't dying. "Hobe!" he said.

Hobe looked briefly at Ashel, and his head picked up the rolling and his tongue the moaning. He had people listening to him; he was an important man tonight.

Ashel seized his shoulder. "You're going to talk to me, Hobe. Or I will hurt you."

Hobe said in a whimpering voice, "A man can't even die in peace."

Ashel's fingers bit deeper. A man didn't die of a broken leg. "What happened? I want the truth, Hobe."

Hobe sucked in his breath, and terror was on his face. "Dandy Cabe ran me down with his horse. He tried to kill me. I saw it in his face. Vaughan sent him. He wanted me killed. I was only the first. He'll pick us off, one by one."

"Shut up," Ashel said furiously. Running a man down with a horse wasn't the surest method of killing him. If Vaughan had something like that in mind, he would have ordered a different method. If Hobe wasn't lying, then Cabe did this on his own, out of pure cussedness.

"You sure it was Cabe? Who was with him?"

"It was Cabe," Hobe said shrilly. "I've seen him enough in town to know him. I didn't know the other one."

Ashel let go his shoulder, and Hobe resumed his moaning. Ashel stepped out of the alcove, and the curtains fell together behind him.

Paw said in a shocked voice, "Talking to your brother like that, when he's hurt so bad."

Ashel didn't look at him. "Nobby," he snapped. "What happened?"

Nobby's eyes were sullen. "Just what Hobe told you. We were walking along the road, minding our own business. They came out of nowhere. The two of them. I ran and Hobe ran. Cabe took out after Hobe. My God! I thought Hobe was broken in two. I hid in the trees until they were gone. I don't know why they didn't come after me. I went home and got the wagon and put Hobe in it."

Ashel stared at him. That was fear back of Nobby's eyes. If it was a lie, Nobby and Hobe had invented quite a few details. Ashel decided Nobby wasn't lying.

Reynolds asked, "Now will you believe what's in front of your eyes? Vaughan ordered this. He has to be the one behind all the trouble. If we stay apart like we've been going, he'll get every one of us. I say it's time to band together and move against him. We'll run him out of the country, instead of him running us."

Ashel's eyes were filled with scorn. "You damned fool. Do you believe that?" Vaughan had gone through fire and drought and blizzard. "A dozen or fifty of you can't run Milo Vaughan." A lot of people would be hurt, if the homesteaders followed Reynolds' reckless words. Most of them would be homesteaders. At the first move they made against Vaughan, every cattleman in the country would be behind him.

Thomas scowled at him. "You were right, Clell. I didn't believe it. But he's gone over to them."

Ashel gave him a hot-eyed look. "Milo Vaughan isn't

interested in any land but his own. He didn't order Hobe hurt. Cabe and I have had some trouble. Cabe did it out of pure meanness to get back at me. When Milo hears about it, he'll fire Cabe."

Their faces were unconvinced, and Ashel said, "If he does fire Cabe, won't that prove what I'm saying?"

Reynolds nodded unwillingly. "It might. We can wait a day or two and see what happens."

Ashel turned toward the door. He had a little time, and that was something gained. A dismal thought struck him. Dandy Cabe had been with Vaughan for a long time. Did Vaughan's loyalty reach far enough to cover even this? No, Ashel decided. It did not. Vaughan would never stand for anything like this.

As he stepped outside Elodia was just coming from the shed. Disappointment was on her face. "Is the talking over already?"

"It's over, kid." A touch of grimness was in his voice. She meant tonight's talking, and he hoped that was all that was included. Reynolds and Thomas and all the others were pushing past the talking stage.

"Did you listen to Hobe?" she asked. "Doesn't he sound awful?"

"He's all right." His tone carried no sympathy. He suspected before Hobe recovered he would run the legs off Elodia on one errand after another. He wanted to warn her against it and knew the warning would be wasted. A twelve-year-old would listen to Hobe's groans. The sound would be more convincing than any words Ashel could use.

He said, "You be good. I'll be back soon."

Her face was wistful. "I wish you could stay all the time, Ashel."

Vaughan said flatly, "I don't believe you. Why would Dandy hurt your brother?"

"To get back at me." It was going worse than Ashel expected. In the first place, Millie and Jenny were in the room, and Vaughan would not ask them to leave. It limited the words a man could use.

"You ordered him to stay away from me," Ashel said. "He couldn't let it go at that. He had to find another way."

Vaughan was getting angry. "I never knew Dandy to be a roundabout man. I don't think it now. Give me one solid reason. Just one."

Millie and Jenny looked at each other, and Millie nodded to her daughter.

Jenny said, "Milo, Dandy's jealous of Ashel."

Vaughan stared at her. "Why?"

Jenny looked at the floor. "Because of me."

"What the hell's going on here?" Vaughan roared. "Compared to you, Dandy's an old man."

Millie's voice was tinged with acid. "You never could see more than a foot beyond your nose. Age has nothing to do with it. Dandy is jealous of Ashel and Jenny being together."

Vaughan's face was confused. "Are you trying to tell me Ashel and Jenny—"

Millie said impatiently, "Ashel knows Jenny is to be married. She told him."

Vaughan said heavily, "I can see one thing. You're all against Dandy. I'll get him in here, and we'll find out what's been going on."

Ashel didn't want Cabe in this room, but he couldn't protest. He sat tight-lipped while Vaughan walked to the door and roared, "Dandy. Come in here."

He came back and put a glowering look on the three of them. "Now we'll see."

Cabe came into the room. If he was worrying, it didn't show in his face. "What do you want, Milo?"

"Ashel claims you rode his brother down." Vaughan was a direct man. He always went straight to the heart of a matter.

"Why, the goddamned liar." Cabe looked at the women. "Excuse me. I couldn't help that. When was this supposed to have happened?"

"Yesterday morning," Ashel said. A worry began to eat at him. How was he going to prove that Cabe was lying? Would Vaughan take Hobe's and Nobby's word against Dandy's?

"Where was it supposed to be?" A glint of malicious amusement was in Cabe's eyes.

"On the road a couple of miles from my family's house. Both my brothers swear it was you."

"They're liars. I can prove where I was." Cabe looked at Vaughan. "Can I call Pete and Lanny in?"

"Anything to get this cleared up," Vaughan growled.

Cabe stepped to the door and called Pete and Lanny. They came into the room, and Ashel was positive he saw the vestige of a grin on their faces. This isn't bothering them, he thought. They look like they expected to be called in. The worry ate deeper into him.

"Lanny. Pete," Cabe ordered. "Tell Milo where I was

yesterday morning."

"You were with us." Pete looked solemnly at Vaughan. Lanny nodded in confirmation.

"Where?" Vaughan asked.

"At Snake Gulch," Lanny said. "Dandy thought we might've missed some stock when we moved them the other day. He was right. We combed it and raised six head. We didn't get in until almost suppertime."

It wasn't hard to guess Vaughan's thoughts. Snake Gulch was a good fifteen miles away in the opposite direction from Ashel's house. A man couldn't be in two spots at once.

Vaughan's eyes were frosty as he stared at Ashel. "That's all, Dandy," he said.

Cabe followed Pete and Lanny to the door, then came back. "Milo, can I say something?"

"Say it, Dandy?"

"Ask him if the two men who set the fire weren't his brothers. I think one of them got hurt trying to get off your land. I don't know what they've got in mind, but I'll bet it winds up with the sodbusters blaming you for it. Maybe the Honyocker's family are the ones pushing the trouble against us."

"That's a lie," Ashel said hotly.

"Were your brothers the ones who set that fire?" Cabe asked softly.

Every eye in the room was upon Ashel. He wanted to deny it and knew it would do no good. His expression was giving him away.

"Yes," he said miserably. "They set it. I rode home night before last to talk to them. I scared them enough so that they'll never try anything like that again." He put a pleading look on Vaughan. "Milo, the two things aren't tied in together. Cabe rode Hobe down. He knows the reason he did it. I don't think it was because of the fire."

Vaughan's eyes darkened. His voice was ominously quiet. "You expect me to believe that, after what Lanny and Pete said? I'm to believe you against the three of them?"

Ashel said bitterly, "They had their story all ready before they came in. It was written all over their faces. I know this, Milo. If Cabe gets away with this, the homesteaders will band against you." The moment it was out he wished he hadn't said it. It only further inflamed Vaughan.

"Are you threatening me?" Vaughan demanded.

"I know what I'd do, if it was me," Cabe said. "I'd throw him off the place."

Vaughan whirled on him. "When I want you to tell me what to do, I'll ask you. That's all, Dandy."

Cabe wore an injured air. "All right, Milo. I was only trying to help."

He looked back at Ashel from the door. Ashel could swear a grin was behind that sober countenance.

Millie waited until the door closed. "Milo, there's something funny about all this."

Her resistance further enraged him. "Are you saying I should believe him against three of my men? Men who have been with me for years?"

His anger struck a responsive spark in Millie. "I'm telling you not to bull your neck before you know what's going on. I've seen you get stubborn before. Dandy has tried to get rid of Ashel every way he could. I think he's still working at it."

"That's loyalty," Vaughan shouted. "You know how long Dandy has been with us. You know what he's done."

She said acidly, "I also know a man can change if he's crossed often enough. Dandy's been crossed."

"That's enough, Millie," Vaughan roared.

Ashel didn't want a family quarrel starting because of him. "Milo, I think I'd better go."

Vaughan's face was cold. "I think so, too. There's been too much trouble since you came."

Millie was speechless for a moment, then she shook her finger at Vaughan. "You talk about loyalty. Are you forgetting how this place looked before Ashel came?"

Vaughan's neck was a fiery red. "We got along before he came. We'll get along after he goes."

"Milo," Millie said, "if you don't talk to Ashel's brothers, if you don't make every attempt to learn all you can about this, I swear I'll never speak to you." She turned and left the room.

Vaughan stared after her, a defeated look on his face. He realized his lacerated feelings were showing, and he looked at Ashel. "You satisfied with the trouble you made?" he asked harshly.

Jenny said, "I never thought I'd see the day when my father was unfair. Ashel, I want to talk to you. Outside."

She made the last word an insult, and Vaughan winced. "Jenny," he said. "I'm ordering you to stay here."

She gave him a contemptuous glance and walked to the door. Vaughan's mouth opened and closed, then he stared at the floor.

When they were outdoors, Ashel said, "Jenny, I don't want to be the cause of trouble. If I could talk to Millie and tell her—"

"No," she said firmly. "Milo will calm down when he's had time to think things over. Millie staying mad at him will push him along. Give him time, Ashel."

He felt a mournful satisfaction in the thought that Millie and Jenny believed him. He said, "I was thinking of leaving the country."

Jenny gripped his arm. "My wedding's in four days. I wanted you to be there. Promise me you'll stay that long."

He wanted to refuse her and he couldn't. "I'll stay that long."

She leaned over and kissed him on the cheek. "It'll be all right, Ashel. You wait and see." The false brightness in her voice couldn't quite cover the doubt.

He waited until she entered the house before he moved. He had grown to love these people, this place. Yesterday he had firm ground under his feet and now there was nothing. Vaughan wouldn't change his mind. And two angry women would only make him more stubborn. Ashel wished he hadn't given his promise to Jenny.

He moved toward the bunkhouse. He had a few personal belongings he wanted to gather. He couldn't take Blackie with him. It was going to be a long walk home.

CHAPTER SIXTEEN

"I'm glad you're back, Ashel," his mother said.

Paw shook his head in doleful contradiction. "I was counting on that money Vaughan paid you to see us through until next spring." His eyes grew fever bright. "We'll make it. We'll tear up more land and put in more wheat. One crop is all we need. We've had so many bad years, we're bound to get a good one next year."

Ashel thought dully, nothing changed. The "now" never mattered to this family. It was always the future. But the "now" would always plague them, and it would always be bad.

He pushed aside his bowl of oatmeal and said, "I'm not hungry."

Nobby sneered, "I guess its not good enough for you."

Ashel checked his denial. He was used to better. He thought of Millie, of the meals she served. He contrasted this squalid kitchen with the one in Vaughan's house; and his throat ached with longing.

From behind the curtains, Hobe groaned, and Maw jumped to her feet to see if she could make him easier. Ashel felt a wild helplessness. Nothing was going to change here, and he was trapped in this meaningless void. I've got to get out of here, he thought. Vaughan's wasn't the only place a man could find work if he wanted it. Again he wished he hadn't promised Jenny.

He pushed to his feet and said, "I'm going outside."

Nobby watched him with speculative eyes, and Paw frowned at him as though he was a stranger. I am, he thought. It didn't take much time for a man's eyes to focus on something better.

He walked to the shed and stared gloomily at it. If it wasn't straightened and braced this summer, the winter winds would flatten it. He couldn't do a thing about it. He needed tools and material.

The morning dragged away, and he thought, it's going to be hard to kill four days this way. He didn't go into the house for the noon meal. In some manner, each of his family would pull at him. Nobby would be hostile, Maw would show her confused worry, and Paw would whine at him. Only Elodia would remain the same. A twelve-year-old wasn't old enough to be other than simple and direct.

He was sitting under a tree, half dozing, when the sound of hoofs jerked him into awareness. He peered down the road and saw the woman rider. For an instant, the wild hope flooded him that it was Jenny or Millie, that Vaughan had calmed down and was reasoning again, that Vaughan was sending for him. The hope faded. If Vaughan had changed his mind, he wouldn't send either of them. He would come himself.

The horse drew nearer, and he recognized Cassie. He hadn't thought much about her—not since Jenny came. He felt a kind of confused shame. How did he act toward her? What did he say?

Her face was timid as she pulled up and dismounted. "Hello, Ashel."

"Hello, Cassie." He could not help his voice being gruff. She's changed, he thought. The immature lines of her face seemed to have hardened, and he wondered why. He saw hurt deep in her eyes and knew the answer. A person could be ground fine against the hard stone of hurt.

"How have you been, Cassie?"

She gave him a false smile. "Just fine, Ashel. And you?"

He nodded. This was useless conversation, but neither knew how to talk to the other any more.

She caught her breath, then said quickly, "Ashel, you never tried to see me again." In her way, she was as simple and direct as Elodia.

It caught him off balance, and he tumbled for words. He said helplessly, "Cassie, you know what Clell said."

She studied him, and he was touched by the grave sweetness in her face. "That wouldn't have stopped me, Ashel. I'd have come to you any time you asked me."

He couldn't look at her, and he muttered, "Sometimes a man can't do much about things. Things change, whether or not he wants them to."

She made a small sound, and he thought there was anguish in it. But when he looked at her, her face was composed.

He said, "You oughtn't to be here now. Clell would be mad as hell if he found you."

"I'm not afraid of him any more." She said it with such quietness that he knew it was so.

He saw the withdrawing in her face and was suddenly struck with a terrible, desolate loneliness.

She said, "Clell said you'd be back here. I wanted to talk to you. There's bad trouble ahead, Ashel. Clell's been talking to too many people. There was a dozen at our house when I left. What are they doing, Ashel?"

He said grimly, "Making the biggest mistake of their lives." He was a man caught in a rushing river. He could see both banks, but he was carried along so swiftly he could touch neither of them. Clell Reynolds would be riding here to see if Vaughan fired Dandy Cabe. Ashel felt a great helplessness. Reynolds was wrong and Vaughan was wrong, and he could make neither see it.

He said, "Cassie, don't be here when Clell comes."

That flash of anguish appeared in her eyes, then she said woodenly, "All right, Ashel. I just thought you ought to know."

She moved toward her horse, then stopped. She wanted to say something, he saw her struggling with it, then she was moving again.

He wished he could answer that unspoken appeal, but the personal response in him was beaten and battered until it was lifeless.

He was still out in the yard two hours later when Reynolds and a dozen men rode into it. It looked like a war party, and Ashel thought dully, he's got them thinking his way.

Paw and Nobby stood in the doorway. Paw's face was frightened.

Reynolds kept moving his horse toward Ashel, and Ashel thought he was going to push the animal over him. He stood his ground, and when Reynolds stopped his horse, its muzzle touched Ashel's chest.

Reynolds stared at him with hot eyes. "Well?" he demanded harshly.

"What do you want, Clell?" Ashel knew, but he needed time for the right words to come into his mind.

Reynolds swore at him. "You know why I'm here. Did he fire Cabe?"

Ashel could say "Yes" and buy a little time, but Reynolds would learn the truth. He looked at the hard-faced men bunched behind Reynolds. He used to call all of them friends, but that was dead now.

He shook his head. "Cabe denied it to Milo. Milo believed him."

He saw the fire leaping in Reynolds' eyes and cried, "Clell, Milo has nothing to do with it. He believed Cabe because he's worked for him a long time. If I take you there, will you talk to him?"

"No." The word was as savage as a hammer blow. "I will not beg from any of them."

"It wouldn't be begging, Clell. Two men, if they want to, can talk out their differences."

Reynolds looked at Paw. "Backus," he ordered. "Come out here."

Paw came reluctantly into the yard.

"He's one of them, Backus. Vaughan sent him over here to find out what we're doing. Throw him off the place."

Paw glanced from Reynolds to Ashel, and he swallowed hard.

Reynolds' face was implacable. "You're with us or you're against us, Backus. Make your pick."

His mother heard the words, for Ashel heard her wail coming from inside the house. He saw his father's face, twisting in fear and indecision. His father was a weak man, caught up in forces he couldn't cope with.

He said, "It's all right, Paw. I'm going."

He turned back to Reynolds. "Clell, you're going to get a lot of people hurt. You start this, and—"

"Get," Reynolds interrupted. He moved his horse forward, and this time Ashel knew he would force the animal over him.

He turned and walked away. He looked back after a dozen strides. All of them were watching him. He thought he heard his mother sob. This was loneliness at its lowest depth.

Reynolds said, "I talked to Pastor Clements this morning.

He's marrying Vaughan's daughter to some Easterner. The wedding's going to be in town. That's the time to hit them."

Heads bobbed in agreement. Suge Thomas said, "They won't be looking for trouble. They won't be carrying guns to a wedding."

Reynolds' eyes bored into Paw. "Backus, I'll expect you and Nobby to meet us in town Thursday morning."

Paw pulled at his fingers. "Somebody's got to stay with Hobe," he objected.

"You got womenfolks for that. You trying to back out on us?"

"No, no," Paw said quickly.

Nobby leaned forward, his face fierce and predatory. "Get Ashel, too. He's one of them."

CHAPTER SEVENTEEN

Cabe's face was a mask showing no emotion. Behind it was the bewilderment, the frozen hurt that no amount of liquor could thaw. He banged his fist upon the table, and the glasses jumped. The bottle would have overturned if Pete had not caught it.

"They could've told me," Cabe mumbled. They waited until yesterday morning, then invited everyone to come into town for Jenny's wedding, her wedding to someone else.

Pete's face had a wise look. "I suspected something like this when that dude showed up three days ago. Didn't you see the way she looked at him?"

"Shut up." Cabe fixed him with terrible eyes.

Pete's mouth opened but no sound came from him.

Lanny kept his eyes fixed on the table. Dandy must be

hurting pretty bad.

"They turned her against me," Cabe said. The "they" was a broad loop including Millie and Milo and the Honyocker. He poured another drink and gulped it down. A dribble of whisky ran down his chin.

Pete watched with fascinated eyes. Cabe could handle more whisky than any man he ever saw.

"I taught her everything." Cabe spoke as though he was unaware the other two were at the table. "She used to follow me around wherever I went." He half closed his eyes, and a shiver ran through him. "Pete, you remember how she followed me around?"

"I remember, Dandy."

Lanny couldn't look at him. It wasn't very pleasant watching another man's suffering. My God, he thought. I didn't know Dandy was such a fool about her. If Dandy didn't stop this hard drinking, he would never get to Jenny's wedding. He'd be stretched out on the floor of this saloon.

"They told her lies," Cabe said. "That's what happened. She couldn't find her way through all those lies."

Lanny could have pointed out that Jenny met Henry Wilcox back East, that there was no one around to lie about Cabe to her. He was smart enough to keep his mouth shut.

Cabe stood and lurched. He slapped a palm against the tabletop to steady himself. The slight lurch and the fixed glassiness of his eyes were the only things telling how drunk he was.

He said, "Stay here until I get back." He bellowed at the bartender, "Hovey, bring them another bottle."

Pete asked, "Where are you going, Dandy?"

Cabe looked at him with surprised eyes. "Why, to see Jenny and tell her about all the lies."

"Dandy," Pete yelped. "The wedding's less than an hour away. She won't listen to you. She—" He subsided as Lanny kicked him under the table.

Cabe's face turned raw and violent. "She'll listen to me," he said and strode out of the saloon. He didn't see Lanny shake his head at Pete; he didn't hear Pete say, "Lanny, I guess we need that other bottle."

Cabe didn't reel as he moved down the walk. But his weight came down hard on his heels, making the walk drum. So Pete thought she wouldn't listen to him. Pete didn't know her very well. She was Dandy Cabe's woman, and nothing could change that.

He entered the lobby of the Montana Hotel and moved to the desk. "Yes, Mr. Cabe?" the clerk asked.

Cabe frowned at him. He should know the man's name, but he couldn't pick it out of the fog in his mind. "Is Miss Jenny in her room?"

The clerk nodded. "Room ten. But I don't know whether you ought to—"

Cabe stared at him. "You don't know what?"

"Nothing, Mr. Cabe," the clerk said hastily. He watched Cabe climb the stairs. It was none of his affair, but Cabe shouldn't be going to her room now.

Cabe moved down the hall, peering at the numbers. Ten. This was it. He pounded on the door. He pounded again without giving her time to answer the first knock.

Jenny opened the door, and her face was indignant. Something froze her features at the sight of him. "Dandy," she cried. "You shouldn't be here now."

She wore a light robe, and it followed the curves of her body. Her hair was fixed a different way, piled high on her head, and he had never seen her more beautiful. The ache in his throat was more than he could bear. He looked over her shoulder and saw the wedding dress stretched out on the bed. The sickness inside him was a terrible thing.

She pushed at him and said, "Dandy, get out of here. Millie will be back any minute."

He shoved her aside with a sweeping arm and entered the room. "I've got to talk to you, Jenny. You don't know what you're doing."

He was very drunk, and fright touched her. She had never taken Ashel's advice and talked to Dandy. She had taken the easy way out and avoided him. She knew now it was a mistake. She had always known Dandy was an intense person, and now with the liquor driving him, he could be dangerous.

She said, "Dandy, please go. I'll talk to you after the wedding."

It was the wrong thing to say, for his eyes flamed. "No wedding," he said thickly. "You're my girl. They told you lies about me. All lies." He kicked the door shut behind him.

Indignation firmed her face. "Dandy, get out of here, or I'll call—"

He sneered at her threat. "Who will you call? Your Eastern dude? Or the Honyocker?"

She would not call Henry if she could. He would be no match for Dandy in any way, and she found no lack of respect in the thought. But she wished Ashel or Milo were here.

She remembered the years she tagged after this man, and she wanted to be kind as she could. But this was getting embarrassing, and her patience was wearing thin.

"Dandy, if Milo learns you were here like this—"

He lunged for her, and a grasping hand seized her wrist. "You're going to tell Milo you want me here. You're going to tell him you made a mistake."

She could not free her wrist, and she slapped him hard, hoping the shock would jar some sense into his head. She was still not seriously frightened. She kept thinking how embarrassing this would be if Henry learned of it.

"Dandy, if you don't let go of me and get out of here, I'll kill you, myself."

That tickled him and he threw back his head and laughed. "That's the gal I taught," he said. He suddenly pulled her to him, and his mouth sought her lips.

Panic seized her, and she lost her head. She struggled with him, and her resistance further inflamed him. One arm wrapped around her, and a hand pawed her throat. She did not hear the material of her robe rip. She knew rage and fear, and she wanted to kill this man.

The hand clamped on her chin, and she couldn't move her head. His mouth came nearer, and his breath reeked of whisky.

"You kiss Dandy," he said. "And you'll forget your dude."

She thought wildly, if he kisses me I'll vomit. She went limp in his arms, letting her weight hang against them. He looked at her closed eyes and said, "Jenny? Jenny, do you hear me?"

The tightness of his grip relaxed, and she pushed hard

against him and tore free. She whirled and ran for the door, her breath sobbing in her throat in fear that his hands would close on her again.

She got it open and glanced over her shoulder. He stood in the middle of the room, a bewildered look on his face.

Her eyes filled with tears at the sight of her father coming down the hall. She blinked them back. She would not let herself cry.

Vaughan saw the torn robe, he saw the emotion twisting her face and said, "Jenny, what the hell's happening?"

She hugged him, wanting the security of his touch. Her words were jerky. "It's Dandy. He forced his way into my room."

Vaughan's eyes blazed, and he said a savage oath. He pushed her from him and strode into the room. Cabe hadn't moved. Either his muscles lacked power to move him or his mind refused to give the orders.

He recognized the menace in Vaughan's face, for he backed and threw up a hand. "Now wait, Milo. I only wanted to talk to her."

Vaughan cursed him with an intensity Jenny had never heard before. He brushed aside the upheld hand and smashed Cabe in the face. The blow knocked Cabe backwards, and he would have gone down without the wall's support. He had three handicaps—he was drunk, he was up against the boss and, worst of all, Vaughan's terrible rage. He had never seen Milo look like this before.

"Wait," he said again. "You wouldn't let me talk to her. You let her listen to everyone else. I didn't get my chance. I didn't—"

"You drunken bastard. Even if she wanted you, do you

think I'd let you have her?"

The words froze Cabe's mind. From somewhere far off, he heard a thin, distant wailing of protest and did not realize it came from within him. He saw the intent in Vaughan's eyes, and he could not raise his arms to protect himself. He wasn't good enough for her. That was the only thought he could get a hold of.

Vaughan sledged him in the face again, and it was an explosive, shocking thing, jerking Cabe off his feet. Oddly enough, he felt no pain, at least, no outward pain.

He lay on the floor, looking up at Vaughan, unaware of the blood that ran from the corner of his mouth.

"You're through," Vaughan raged. "Pack your stuff and get off my place. If I ever see you around again I'll kill you."

He stood over Cabe, his chest heaving. Jenny thought he was going to kick Dandy, and she ran to him and seized his arm.

"Don't," she said.

He looked at her, and his eyes cleared. A heavy, defeated quality came into his face, and his shoulders drooped. "Ashel was right about him," he muttered. "At least, part of it."

"Maybe more," she said.

Vaughan sighed. "Maybe," he admitted. "I've got to find out."

He looked at Cabe. "Dandy, get out of here. Now." He started to reach for Cabe, and Jenny's hand restrained him.

Cabe dragged himself to his feet. His mind was a frozen thing, an icy void moving him without volition. A name slipped into it. She said, "Ashel" and Vaughan agreed with her. The Honyocker was the cause of all his troubles. The Honyocker! It beat against his head like the smash of a club. He moved woodenly toward the door. Behind him he heard Jenny say, "Milo, talk to Ashel. He promised to be here for my wedding."

Vaughan said heavily, "I will, Jenny. I will."

Cabe stopped at the door and looked back at them. It was odd he felt no hatred for them. It all went to the Honyocker. He had none to spare for anyone else.

"Close the door," Vaughan ordered. He didn't want anyone passing down the hall and looking into this room. What was he going to tell Millie? That question worried him most of all.

As Cabe pulled the door after him, he heard Jenny say, "Milo, I want another room."

"Sure, honey," Vaughan said. "I understand."

The catch clicked behind Cabe, and he moved toward the steps. The hatred was a roaring flame in his mind. The Honyocker was going to be in town. He would find him if he had to tear every building apart.

CHAPTER EIGHTEEN

Ashel was a mile from town when the buggy overtook him. He stepped to the side of the road to let it pass. He did not expect a lift. He couldn't put his finger on a single friend in all this country.

The buggy stopped, and Ashel stubbornly kept his back turned toward it. He wasn't begging a favor from anyone.

"Ashel."

He turned at the sound of his name. Cassie Reynolds

looked at him with red-rimmed eyes. He knew she had been crying, and he had the uncomfortable feeling he was the cause of it.

He moved to the buggy and asked, "What's wrong, Cassie?"

"It's Clell," she said and swallowed hard.

He thought she was going to cry, but she blinked several times and the tears did not come.

"He's bound on forcing trouble, Ashel. Men have been coming and going at our house for the last two days. The night before last I heard them talking. Clell said, 'They won't expect us to hit them at the wedding.' Do you know what he means?"

Ashel kept a blank face. He knew what Reynolds meant. The last thing Vaughan would expect today would be something like Reynolds was planning. Reynolds might sweep the town free of cattlemen today. Perhaps he hoped to catch enough of them there to break the back of their resistance. But he was wrong. He might cripple them, but he couldn't smash them. Cattlemen would ride in from all over the country to strike back in bloody retaliation. Ashel thought of Jenny. She was entitled to this day. He thought of Milo and Millie, all caught in a bloody, senseless struggle, a struggle that could only end in savage loss for both sides.

He said, "I don't know what Clell has in mind," and his voice sounded unnatural. He didn't want to pull Cassie into this. He wanted her to stay as far away as possible from it.

She said, "I looked for you all day yesterday, Ashel. Your family didn't know where you were, and neither did Mrs. Vaughan."

She had covered a lot of ground. He said, "I was up in the hills the last couple of days." He had spent them in lonely meditation, trying to see a road ahead of him. He only stayed around here because of his promise to Jenny. Now he had been given another reason. He had to find Vaughan and warn him of the danger. He thought, I'll make him listen to me.

Cassie asked, "Is there going to be a wedding today?" He nodded, and she asked, "Whose?"

"Jenny Vaughan's. She's marrying somebody from the East."

His voice must have carried something, for she gave him a queer glance. "I saw her in town last year. She's pretty, isn't she?"

He thought of Jenny, and the hurt wasn't quite dead. He said woodenly, "Yes."

Something hurt her, for she turned her face. Without looking at him she said, "I'll give you a lift into town."

He said, "No, Cassie." It would be best if she were not seen with him. He looked at the double-barreled shotgun leaning against the edge of the seat and asked, "Are you so afraid you think you need that gun?"

"It's not mine." Her voice sounded as though it wanted to break. "Clell must have put it in the buggy last night, then forgot about it. I just didn't take it out."

"Cassie, don't give it to him. Even if he asks for it." A shotgun was a terrible weapon. "Don't give it to any of them."

"I won't," she promised. She lifted the reins. "Ashel."

He wished she would look at him. He waited, then said, "Yes?"

181

"Nothing." The break was in her voice. She snapped the reins across the horse's rump, and the animal lunged forward.

He stared after the buggy for a long time. That lonely feeling was with him again.

He walked on into town, and as he approached Criss's livery stable, he saw four men in front of it. They fell silent as he neared them, and a hostility molded their faces as they looked at him. He knew them all, little men trying to hold onto their small parcels of land. A tenseness was in them, a tenseness that waiting for a moment of violence produces. Had Reynolds set the time?

He did not attempt to speak to them, and none of them spoke as he passed. He could feel their eyes boring into his back. A sense of urgency seized him, making him want to break into a run. He had to find Milo Vaughan; he had to make him listen.

Every street corner had its knot of homesteaders. They were scattered all over town, and that tenseness was in every one of them. He thought, my God! Would Clell be crazy enough to set up a massacre? He argued against the thought, but it would not leave him.

He passed Emorey's saloon on the other side of the street, and Pete stood in the doorway. Pete gave him a long, hard look before he stepped back.

Ashel quickened his stride. It looked as though Pete stepped back to report to someone. It would probably be Cabe, and the least Cabe would do would be to give him verbal abuse. He hurried on, expecting to hear his name yelled from behind him.

Where would he find Vaughan? At the church? In one of

the saloons, doing some early celebrating? He could spend a lot of time finding him. Maybe too much time. The hotel flashed into his mind. Millie or Jenny should be there, even if Vaughan wasn't. They could tell him where to look.

He was a half block from it, passing the mouth of an alley, when he saw Cabe coming out of the hotel door. He checked his stride and pulled back into the alley. Cabe surely knew by now. He would be in a nasty temper, and he would take that temper out on Ashel. He might stop him entirely from getting to Vaughan.

He moved twenty yards deep into the alley. His heart pounded as he pressed against the wall of a building. He was in shadow, and he hoped Cabe would pass the mouth of the alley without seeing him. The sound of boot heels grew louder on the walk, and Ashel prayed, don't look this way.

Cabe passed the alley, and the sound of his steps faded. Ashel waited a few more minutes. Cabe came out of the hotel. It was likely that Vaughan was there.

He walked into the lobby and asked the man behind the desk. "Is Milo Vaughan here?"

Belligerence rode the clerk's thin face. "He's here. He won't see you. He won't see anybody right now. He was just down here and gave me orders not to let anybody go upstairs. I don't know what happened, but he's sore about something." He took an indignant breath. "He took it out on me. Like it was my fault."

Ashel's eyes were worried. It was going to be difficult to talk to Vaughan at best. If he was on the warpath, it could be impossible. He wondered what had riled Milo. Probably some report Cabe had just brought him. Maybe Vaughan already knew about the homesteaders gathered in town. But Ashel had to be sure. Should he wait in the lobby? It might be an hour before Vaughan came down. It might be better to wait outside, where he could sort of watch things. It might be possible to talk to Clell Reynolds, though he doubted it. Two hard-headed men aligned against each other, and he was caught between them.

He walked outside, and traffic in the street seemed to have grown heavier. Three riders raced down the street, whooping as they rode. A wedding was a big day, a day of skylarking. The dust from their passage settled over a group of hard-eyed, bitter men. Ashel saw the way the men stared after the riders. Just a little thing could trigger this into explosive madness.

CHAPTER NINETEEN

Pete looked up just as Cabe pushed through the swinging doors. A wash of sunlight bathed Cabe's face, and Pete saw the harsh molding of it. He also saw the bruise on Cabe's mouth and the spot of fresh blood.

He said, "Dandy ran into trouble," and started to rise.

Lanny said, "Sit down." He knew Cabe's temper when he looked like this. "Let him talk about it."

Cabe sat down without speaking to either of them. He poured and drank three shots in rapid succession, and his eyes were wild.

"The son of a bitch," he said and smashed the glass on the floor.

"Who?" Pete asked. He shrank back under the hard impact of Cabe's eyes.

Cabe cursed Ashel without naming him. "He turned Millie against me. She worked on Milo. Now Jenny won't even talk to me." In his drunken mind he found no particular blame against Vaughan. None of this would have happened if the Honyocker had not come along.

"You mean the Honyocker," Pete said with relief.

Cabe's face twisted. "I'm going to kill him. I'm going to ride out to his place and cut him down."

"You won't have to ride any place," Pete said. "He's here in town."

"You lying to me?"

"I saw him. Not over five minutes ago. Going down the other side of the street."

Cabe remembered Jenny saying the Honyocker would be here for the wedding. Pete could be right. He seized the bottle and drank deeply from it. He stood and asked, "You two want to come along and see me shoot a rabbit?" The whisky's weight was drowning most of the hurt. He could even convince himself that killing the Honyocker would erase all of it.

Lanny took a long drink and said, "Sure." His eyes shone with recklessness. Pete was already on his feet.

Cabe frowned at him. "He's mine. Just remember that."

He went out the door a step ahead of them. "Which way was he going?" he asked.

Pete pointed down the street.

The three of them filled the walk. A man coming toward them had the impulse to argue about it—until he saw their expressions. Then he stepped hastily into the street. At the corner, they passed a group of homesteaders. The two groups exchanged hard stares, and Lanny bristled. He looked back after he passed them and said, "Dandy, we ought to run all the bastards out of town."

The whisky was enveloping Cabe in a warm wave. Only the pinpoint of his determination rode above it. "Maybe we will, Lanny. After we get him."

Pete stopped and gripped Cabe's arm. "There he is, Dandy. At the end of the hotel porch."

Cabe didn't need Pete's pointing. He saw the damned Honyocker. He said, "Ah," and it was a wicked, animal sound.

He filled his lungs and roared, "You."

The Honyocker's head jerked this way. Cabe drew his gun. It was a long shot, too long for accuracy. He fired, and the Honyocker was galvanized into motion. He ran toward the alley near the hotel and disappeared into it.

Cabe laughed. He hadn't wanted to hit him with that shot.

Lanny said, "You warned him too soon, Dandy."

"I wanted to. I wanted to see him run."

"He's liable to get away from us," Lanny complained.

Cabe shook his head. "He can't run fast enough to get away from me."

Ashel was panting hard by the time he came out of the alley. He hesitated in fearful indecision, glancing to his right and left, then behind him. He was unarmed and friendless, and three men hunted him. Cabe wouldn't let it go with just the one shot. He would hunt Ashel down like an animal, and the next shot wouldn't miss. Panic churned in his mind. He had the impulse to blind flight, and he forced himself to think. He was on foot, and if he left the security of the town for open country, he would be spotted before he covered a quarter mile. If he had a horse, he might make a break for it, but the horses were all tied along the main street. He wouldn't hesitate to steal one if he thought he had the time. His face brightened. He might get a horse from the livery stable.

He drew a deep breath and turned to his left, keeping as close to the buildings as he could. His mouth was dry, and his nerves jerked. This was the feeling of being hunted. It made a man's skin icy, and he breathed in painful gasps. He came to the end of the block, and paused, afraid to look around the corner.

He peered around the building's edge. No one was in the block. He was two blocks from the livery stable. He could reach it in a few seconds if he had the nerve to dash for it. He debated it, then decided it would be best to take it as slow as he could. A running man would attract the most attention. He looked behind him, and it was clear. How difficult it was for a man to cover all directions at once.

He stepped out onto the walk, and his heart was a misplaced mass, blocking his breathing. Cabe had just turned the corner and was moving toward him. He yelled and fired at the same time, and Ashel heard the thwock of a bullet hitting a building wall.

He spun and ran back around the corner. If Pete or Lanny had come through the alley, he was trapped. He dared not run as far as the alley, and he slipped into a three-foot opening between two buildings. He ran hard down the dark lane, and a tin can turned under his foot. He stumbled and almost lost his balance. He threw a hand against a building side, steadying himself. He made his decision as he ran. He would cross the main street in a burst of speed, hoping that if they were waiting for him, the unexpectedness would throw them off.

A man was coming down the walk as Ashel burst out onto it, and he almost ran him down. He pushed hard against the man, sending him staggering. For an instant he had been afraid it was one of them, and the fear wanted to pull a scream out of him. He raced across the street, seeking an exit between buildings on the other side. He found it between The Emporium and Halsey's restaurant and slipped into it. He heard a cry coming from somewhere along the street and did not know who made it. Fear was a terrible sickness. It put the sour taste of vomit in a man's mouth, and each breath sent a stabbing thrust through his lungs. He turned the corner of The Emporium, and flattened against the back wall, trying to ease the pumping of his lungs.

Somewhere behind him, they were hunting him—or were they before him? He was naked in an uncaring world, and his eyes stung. He swallowed hard, pushing the weakening sickness aside. If he could just reach the livery stable, old man Criss would give him a horse.

He moved slowly down the rear of the line of buildings, his eyes darting forward and back. Ahead of him, he had a side street to cross. Should he run for it or try to slip furtively across it? He stopped and looked around the corner. The street was clear. He decided to run for it.

He raced across the street and pounded down the next block. He had to skirt a pile of tin cans, and a dog came out of a building and barked at him. Ashel cursed the dog. He swung a kick at it and missed. The animal danced around him, barking louder. He ran on, fearful that the dog would pull attention to him. It followed him across three back yards, then stopped. The last building on the block was a house, and a woman stood in the doorway watching him. He caught just a glimpse of her face as he passed, and it looked startled.

He crossed the next street and was in back of the livery stable. He stepped into the building, and as the walls closed about him a tearing sob of relief escaped him.

He moved between the double line of box stalls, smelling the pungent odor of manure. The stalls were filled, he supposed because of Jenny's wedding. Any one of these animals could take him safely away from town.

Criss stood in the doorway, looking out into the main street. He held a rifle in his hand, and Ashel wondered why.

He crept to within twenty feet of the man, then hissed at him. Criss whirled, alarm tightening his face.

Ashel motioned for him to leave the door, and Criss moved with reluctance. His old, lined face was strained. Some fear had brushed him.

He stopped a good two strides from Ashel. He said shrilly, "Get out of my place."

"I need a horse, Criss. I need one bad."

"You get no horse here." The old man's eyes touched Ashel's face, then moved in furtive shame. He mumbled, "I got no horses to rent. Every horse here belongs to someone. I'd get skinned if I let you have any one of them."

Ashel caught the shame in Criss's eyes, the lie in his words. "Cabe's been here," he said dully. Cabe would think of this, wanting to keep Ashel on foot.

The accusation raked Criss, and his voice climbed a notch. "What if he has? You're not pulling me into your quarrel with him."

"He's trying to kill me. I haven't got a gun. I need a horse to get out of town." Ashel didn't want the begging note in his voice, but it was there.

"He'd kill me if I gave you a horse. He said so. I know Dandy Cabe. I've seen him—" He shook his head and didn't finish. His grip on life was shaky, and he was going to do nothing to loosen it.

He could not stand Ashel's eyes, and he yelled, "Go on. Take your quarrel outside."

Ashel cursed him with every oath at his command. Criss's face reddened, but he just stood there, shaking his head, his eyes not meeting Ashel's.

Ashel said, "I can take a horse."

Criss leveled the rifle muzzle on Ashel's chest. "You just try it. Go on. Try it."

Criss meant it. His determination was written all over his face. Ashel looked at the bore of the rifle. He never realized it looked so big from this side.

"At least, give me a gun," he begged.

"No," Criss said doggedly. "I got no part in this. Go on, now. Get out of my place. You go out the front door." The light was poor in the rear of the building, and his eyes were old. Besides, the front door was the closest.

He stepped back to let Ashel pass, and the rifle never wavered.

Ashel moved by him to the entrance. No words were going to shake Criss's stand. A fear gripped him, too.

He looked up and down the street before he stepped out

onto the walk. He could have cried with relief at the sight of Reynolds and Thomas and Wenski standing on the corner.

He ran to them and said, "Clell, let me take your horse. Cabe's after me."

Thomas and Wenski stared at the ground. Reynolds said, "I know. We got no horse for you."

Stunned, Ashel stared at him. Hatred was a form of insanity, and in a way, Reynolds' hatred was as big as Cabe's.

He said in a choked voice, "Clell—"

"Get away from us. I don't give a damn how much you fight among yourselves. Kill each other off, and I'll be tickled to death."

"At least give me a gun."

"We've got only enough guns to protect ourselves." Red was mounting up from Reynolds' collar, and he breathed raggedly.

It was no use appealing to the other two. They wouldn't even look at him. Ashel said, "Goddamn you, Clell," and stopped. It was all so useless cursing Reynolds.

He looked up the street. He would steal the first horse he saw. One was tied before Ramsey's store, and no one was near it.

He ran toward the horse. His boots drummed against the walk, and the pain in his chest was interfering with his breathing. If he could jerk those reins free and mount without anyone stopping him, he would have a chance.

He reached the tie rack just as Lanny came around the far corner. He yelled, "Hey," at the sight of Ashel and fired. The bullet went high overhead. The horse lunged and pulled back to the end of its reins. There would be no time to fight it into submission.

Ashel whirled to retrace his steps. Cabe and Pete were coming around the corner behind him. They had him boxed, and he wanted to scream with the fear. He turned and ran into Ramsey's shop.

Ramsey was standing at the door, and he pulled back to let Ashel enter.

"Give me a gun," Ashel said hoarsely.

Ramsey shook his head. "I haven't got a gun." Truth was in his voice. "Go out the back door."

It was a little enough thing, but tears welled into Ashel's eyes. It was more than any of the others had done for him. He ran toward the back door.

Vaughan heard the second shot as he came out of the hotel. He looked up the street, and people were frozen in curiously strained attitudes. If those gunshots meant menace to them, they wouldn't be on the street. They'd be inside behind closed doors.

Halsey stood before his restaurant, and Vaughan hurried to him. "What's going on?" he asked.

"I'm not sure," Halsey said. "Someone said Cabe's on the warpath. He's trying to shoot one of the homesteaders."

Ashel's name popped into Vaughan's mind. Oh, good God, no, he thought. But it fitted. Cabe would be sucking a monumental hatred, and Ashel would be its most likely target.

"There's Dandy now," Halsey said.

Vaughan saw Cabe step onto the street a half block away. He ran toward him, and Cabe swiveled his head to watch him. Vaughan reached him and drew several breaths before he could speak.

"Dandy, what the hell are you doing?"

Cabe drawled, "I'm hunting me a rabbit. I'm going to kill that goddamned Honyocker."

"Let him alone," Vaughan said sharply.

Cabe's voice was almost a purr. "Why, Milo, you can't be giving me orders. I'm not working for you any more."

Vaughan thought, He's using this as a club to make me crawl. Dandy could have his job back if that was the only way to stop this.

Cabe's eyes filled with meanness. "You sonuvabitch. I know what you're thinking. I wouldn't work for you again if you paid me double. Don't try to stop me from killing him." He swung the gun he was holding. "I'd just as soon kill you as not. Maybe I will after I finish with him."

Vaughan stared at him. Cabe hated good when he was sober. Now he was drunk. Nothing would stop him. Nothing but a gun. For an instant he had the fear Cabe would shoot him. He backed and said, "All right, Dandy. I'm going. I'm not stopping it."

He turned and walked rapidly away, hearing Cabe's laughter behind him. He cursed himself for not having a gun with him. But a gun was the last thing he thought of to bring to Jenny's wedding. But he had to find one; he had to stop Cabe. He broke into a run as he saw Wainright step out of Emorey's saloon.

He reached Wainright, and his rapid breathing made his words jerky. "Travis, give me a gun. Dandy's gone crazy."

Wainright's eyes were bright with interest. "I heard about that. He's hunting that Honyocker who worked for you.

193

The one who put up that ride on Fireball."

Vaughan made an impatient gesture. He knew who Cabe was hunting. "Give me a gun," he repeated.

"Hell, Milo. What would I be doing wearing a gun to Jenny's wedding? And I didn't see one on any of the boys who came in."

Vaughan cursed helplessly. No one would think to wear a gun to town today. No one but Dandy Cabe.

Wainright said, "You could get one from the sodbusters. You notice how many of them are in town? All of them armed, too. What are they up to, Milo?"

"I don't know." Vaughan had enough on his mind without worrying about the sodbusters. And it probably would be a waste of time trying to get a gun from any of them. He said, "I'll have to buy a gun." That would take precious seconds, and every second Cabe was hunting Ashel.

Wainright shook his head. "The Emporium's closed. In honor of Jenny. And I just saw Atkins at the bar in here. I suspect his store's closed, too."

Vaughan started through the saloon doors. "He'll open it, then." Atkins would open that store if he had to drag him across the street by the scruff of his neck.

Wainright called after him, "You planning on stopping Dandy?"

"I'm going to try."

Ashel cowered behind the false front on the roof of Ramsey's shop. He had reached the edge of the roof from the alley and swung himself up to it. How long had he been running and hiding? It seemed like an eternity, though maybe it hadn't been longer than thirty minutes. His tongue felt thick in a desert-dry mouth. God, he wished he had a drink.

Twice Cabe had passed below him. Ashel heard him call to Pete and Lanny somewhere up the street. They must have answered with a negative gesture, for Cabe swore before he moved on.

Ashel looked at the sun. It rode high in the sky. It was still a good many hours until dark. Could he remain hidden that long? He was afraid to examine that question honestly.

He heard yelling from the street again, but it was too far away for him to recognize the voice. He hated this town and everyone in it. People watched him running and ducking, and no one offered help of any kind. He changed that. Ramsey offered what help he could. But it was a spectacle to the rest of them, this watching a man being crowded closer and closer to his death. A few minutes ago Cabe had almost gotten him. He passed within a yard of where Ashel crouched under the outside flight of steps leading to the second story above Halsey's restaurant. It was then he thought of the roofs. He might be able to wait out the endless hours there until darkness gave him some slight protection.

The tar-paper roofing absorbed heat and threw it back at Ashel. He squirmed on the hot surface, and his throat grew dryer. He tried to spit, and only wisps of cotton were in his mouth.

Voices yelled back and forth. Then Cabe's voice sounded from right below him. Ashel pressed tighter against the false front, though he knew he couldn't be seen.

"Goddamn it, Pete," Cabe roared. "I know he's in

town someplace."

Pete called, "We've looked in every store, Dandy. We haven't been through the houses yet. Do you think anybody's got enough nerve to try to hide him from you?"

Cabe swore, then suddenly said, "The roofs, Pete. Hell, yes. That's where he's hiding. Climb up on Halsey's restaurant. It's tall enough you can see all the roofs from it."

Ashel tried to swallow and couldn't. The lump stayed in his throat. The trembling started again, worse this time.

He couldn't stay here. Pete would spot him and report to Cabe. He slithered toward the back edge of the roof and dropped into the alley. His knees were treacherous things, momentarily refusing to support him, and he thought he would fall. He braced himself against the wall and closed his eyes. The running was starting again. And he didn't know which step would take him around a corner and straight into Cabe. It would be better to get this torturing suspense over with, it would be better to walk up to Cabe and end it.

He pushed the weak thought aside. He was still alive, and a man hung onto the last agonizing second. He went down the alley. He had a little time. Cabe would wait until Pete surveyed the roofs. Maybe Ashel could find a safer place to hide.

He came out of the alley onto a side street, and his heart gave that sickening bound into his throat again. He wearily shook his head. His nerves must be frazzled if he couldn't recognize Cassie from one of the three who hunted him.

"Ashel," Cassie cried as she saw him. Her cheeks were tear-streaked. "I've been looking all over for you."

"Get away from me," he said fiercely. "Don't you know

what's going on?"

"I know." She thrust the shotgun at him.

He stared at it, and tears came into his eyes. The running was over. He could meet them, meet them with some semblance of a chance.

"Take it," she said. "I couldn't find any extra shells."

He intended to take it. He had forgotten about it being in the buggy. But she hadn't. She was the only one in town who came forward to help him, and something melted in him.

He seized the gun, and the hot feel of the metal was a wonderful thing. She had given him a chance; she had given him his life.

He said gruffly, "Thanks, Cassie. Leave me alone now."

She stared at him with that speechless appeal in her eyes. He leaned forward and kissed her and saw the sweet response in her face.

"Cassie," he said awkwardly. "Thanks for everything."

He cradled the gun and walked toward the corner. He would stand tight against the end building and wait for them to come down the street. He would not step out until then. The ending would be fast and brutal. One way or the other. Fast and brutal.

CHAPTER TWENTY

Ashel didn't know how many minutes had passed, but they moved on leaden feet. He looked around, and Cassie was still there, her face a mask of frozen horror. He scowled at her and shook his head. He kept scowling until she moved away.

The waiting was bad. It was hard for a man to keep himself keyed to this high point. It was hard to keep his nerves and mind directed toward a single second. The dragging time pulled at him, and fear nibbled at the edges of his determination. He didn't know which way they were coming, and that added to the strain. Could he handle the three of them? If they weren't bunched, he couldn't. A shotgun's pattern was broad, but two shells could not reach three men, if they were separated. The worry crawled like snakes through his mind, and he tried to force it blank. But each actual or imagined sound started the snakes slithering again.

He doubted many minutes had passed, though it seemed an hour. His big fear was that someone would see him here, guess his intentions, and report them to Cabe.

He stiffened as he heard voices. They were quarreling voices, and he recognized Cabe's. Who was Cabe talking to? Ashel wished he could see around the corner. Cabe had to be talking to Pete and Lanny. He had to be.

"He's somewhere in town," Cabe said. "I'll tear down every damned building to find him. Pete, are you sure—"

"Dandy, I told you he wasn't on the roofs. I got a good look."

At least Cabe and Pete were around the corner. The voices kept coming nearer, and by the volume of them Ashel tried to figure how far away they were.

Lanny said, "Maybe he slipped out of town on us, Dandy."

Cabe growled, "He didn't. I got a feeling. I know he's someplace near."

That placed all three of them, but the voices no longer

sounded as though they were coming nearer. Ashel was afraid they had stopped. When he stepped around the corner, how far would he be from them? It was a big question. Everything depended upon its answer.

Cabe said, "We'll search the town again."

"Hell, Dandy," Pete said in protest. "I've walked my feet off already."

Cabe cursed him, then abruptly stopped. "I know where he is. Jenny's hiding him in her room. Now why didn't I think of that before?"

The hotel lay in the opposite direction. Should Ashel cut around the block and try to intercept them, or should he step out now? He decided now was as good as he could pick.

He cocked both barrels and drew a deep breath, trying to fill the horrible void in his stomach. He stepped around the corner, the shotgun hip level, and the three were turning to retrace their steps up the street. They were twenty yards away, well within shotgun range.

"Cabe," he said. It came out steady enough.

They whirled, their faces showing varying degrees of surprise. Pete's jaw hung slack, and Lanny struggled with his bewilderment. Cabe recovered first. "You!" he roared.

Pete yelled, "Dandy, he's got a shotgun." His hand clawed for his gun.

Ashel didn't figure the sight of the shotgun would stop them. Nothing but its charge would stop them. Cabe's gun was coming out of its holster, when Ashel pulled the right-hand trigger. The shotgun bucked against his hip, and its blast was unearthly loud. A shotgun charge at twenty yards is a terrible thing. It broke Cabe in the middle and flung him back. In an instant, he went from a living man to an inanimate bundle of clothing. He was dead before he hit the walk. Pete was on Cabe's left, and the edge of the pellets' pattern reached him. Ashel heard him scream and stagger sideways. He went off the walk and bent double over the hitchrack before he slid off it and dropped to the street. His screaming kept ringing in Ashel's ears.

He jerked the muzzle a couple of inches to cover Lanny. Lanny's gun was swinging on him when Ashel pulled the other trigger. The shot blew Lanny apart, and he fell where he stood.

The gun blasts hammered at Ashel's ears, and his mouth and nose were filled with the taste and smell of powder smoke. Pete flopped about in the street, and his screaming would not stop. Cabe and Lanny were horribly torn, and Ashel thought he would vomit.

He stared at them with sickened eyes, and he was incapable of movement. Cries coming from up the street and the sound of pounding feet jerked him out of his trance. He lifted his head, and Vaughan was in the van of the people running toward him. He saw sunlight bounce off the metal of the gun swinging in Vaughan's hand, and a murderous frenzy filled him. It wasn't over. He had to face Vaughan.

He swung the muzzle toward Vaughan, and the frenzy was gone as quickly as it came. He had no shells. And even if he had, he would not fight Milo Vaughan.

He threw the gun from him and said in a dead voice, "Go ahead, Milo."

Vaughan stared at him. "You all right, boy?"

Nothing fitted any more. That was concern in Vaughan's voice. The trembling seized Ashel, and he thought his legs would not support him. He managed to get the shaky words out, "All right, Milo."

Vaughan looked at the shambles that once was his crew. Cabe and Lanny lay on the walk. Pete rolled in the dust of the street, his right hand gripping his shoulder. Blood dripped steadily from between his fingers.

Vaughan's face was grim. "He bought it for himself. I tried to stop him, but I didn't have a gun. By the time I bought one and got here—" A heavy sigh broke into his words and he let them fade.

Ashel could feel the strength flowing back into him. He hadn't known it during all that running, but Vaughan was trying to help him. He knew of another—Cassie—and there were probably others.

Vaughan moved Pete and squatted to examine him. He glanced at Ashel and said, "You got him in the shoulder. He'll live. But he won't use this arm much again."

"Milo, get me to a doctor," Pete moaned.

People were all around them, and more ran toward the scene. Ashel saw Clell Reynolds and Thomas Brosnahan and Wenski were on the other side of the ring. On its far perimeter he saw Cassie. She was shaking uncontrollably, and he tried to smile at her.

Vaughan said, "Ashel, could you forgive a stubborn-headed fool?"

A stinging was back of Ashel's eyes, and he was afraid it would show. "Anybody can make a mistake, Milo."

"A doctor," Pete groaned. "Get me to a doctor."

Vaughan's eyes were merciless. "He should've killed you, too. Now tell me the truth. Did you and Lanny lie for him the other night? Did he run Ashel's brother down?"

Pete looked at him with pain-misted eyes. "Yes, Milo," he said. "It was Dandy. He caused all the trouble. He made me go along with him. Things started going wrong for him when the Honyocker came."

"Why?" Vaughan continued.

Pete spoke weakly. "It fitted Dandy's plan to get the Honyocker out. Dandy wanted to own land. If he had enough land, you'd think he was good enough for Jenny. He picked a sodbuster family at a time and ran them off. He could pick up their land later." Pete closed his eyes. "A doctor, Milo."

Vaughan straightened. "Get this man to Doc Summers," he said.

Four men lifted Pete from the street. Brosnahan and Wenski were two of them. A shame rode their faces, and Ashel thought they wanted to get away.

"Clear the walk," Vaughan said without a glance toward the motionless forms.

Other men picked up Cabe and Lanny. Ashel's eyes were drawn to Cabe's dangling arm. It bounced with every step, the men carrying him, too. The dark stains on the walk were all that was left.

Vaughan faced Reynolds, and his eyes were cold. "Well, Reynolds."

It was difficult for Reynolds to meet Vaughan's eyes. "Well, my God," he burst out. "How was I to know? All I knew was my friends were getting run out. Losing everything they had. Can a man sit still and take that?"

He looked from face to face, and the faces were hostile. Thomas and Slezak looked at him with accusing eyes. Reynolds stood alone.

Ashel said softly, "Milo, a man can make a mistake."

Vaughan glared at him, but a grin twitched at his lip corners.

Reynolds flashed Ashel a grateful glance.

Vaughan said, "It's all over then, Reynolds?"

Reynolds looked at the ground. "I guess it is," he muttered.

Vaughan said, "I'll probably need some hay for the winter, Reynolds."

"You ride over," Reynolds said. "I guess we could make a deal."

Ashel saw the relief lighting Reynolds' face. Reynolds was hardheaded and stubborn, but essentially he was a man of peace. All he wanted was to be left alone to pursue his own way. That was all Vaughan wanted, Ashel thought. That was all any of them wanted. Except a man like Cabe.

The hostility died in the hot street. The suspicion might linger, but time would erase that. At some time in the future there might even be friendship among them. It could be, Ashel thought. They fought a common enemy, the implacable, stubborn land.

"Let me through," Ashel heard Millie say. Men parted to give her way, and she ran up to Ashel. Jenny was behind her, and they hugged and kissed Ashel. Men grinned as they watched, and Ashel felt his face heat. "It's all right," he kept saying. "It's all over."

He looked at Cassie, and she was white-faced. He was sure tears were in her eyes. She looked at Jenny, and an anguish twisted her face. Ashel knew she was making comparisons. She turned to flee, and he had to stop her.

He shouldered through the ring of people and caught her

arm. He said, "Cassie, you're not going any place without me." In the moment she handed him the shotgun, he knew what this woman meant to him, what she had really always meant to him. Jenny? He did not try to explain that, even to himself. He just let her name slip out of his mind. His eyes were anxious as he added, "If you'll let me come along."

An inner radiance began to light her face. A girl was submerged in that growing light, and a woman emerged, a woman secure and confident and beautiful. Why, he thought, she's more beautiful than I ever thought.

She reached for his hand, and her fingers gripped his. "Ashel," she said, and her voice was choked.

Ashel faced the curious people, turning Cassie with him. "Clell," he said. "I'm calling on Cassie."

"I'm going with him, Paw," she said. "Wherever he goes."

People grinned and bobbed their heads. When Reynolds spoke, a heavy, defeated quality was in his voice. He was suffering a loss, and nobody could see it. "I got no objections," he said.

"Fine," Vaughan boomed. "When you two are ready, we'll have the biggest wedding this town ever saw. Ashel, you know that little house near the gate. It'd make a good place to set up housekeeping. I'll get it fixed up real nice."

Ashel's face flamed at all this attention. "But, Milo, I don't even know what I'm going to do."

"Do?" Vaughan asked in surprise. "You're coming back with me." His voice picked up an anxious note. "There's only Tom and me left. I'm going to have to rebuild a crew. I need someone solid to build around. A man can pick up a cow or two as he goes along and before he knows it, he's got a cow herd. Hell, Ashel, you can't be planning on leaving."

Millie took his arm. "Come along, Milo. He needs time to think about it." She looked at Ashel and smiled. "I think I know how he'll decide."

"I'd sure like to know now," Vaughan grumbled. Millie tugged on his arm, and he said, "Come along, everybody. I'll stand a round of drinks, then I got a wedding to attend."

The crowd went down the street, and their talk and laughter grew fainter. Only Jenny remained.

She said, "I'm happy for you." She bent forward quickly and kissed Ashel on the cheek.

He put an anxious glance on Cassie. Her face remained serene.

Jenny looked at Cassie. "You're a lucky woman."

"I know it," Cassie said.

Ashel breathed easier. Something had passed between these two, and they were friends.

Jenny smiled at him and went down the street.

"She's beautiful, Ashel."

"Not as much as you."

She forgot they were standing on a public walk; she forgot the whole town might be watching them. She came to him, and her lips carried all the promise a man could ever want.

He lifted his head and said huskily, "What do you think about what Milo said?" He had the offer of a house and a job. It sounded like a good start to him.

"If you want it," she answered.

He started to say something, and the sound of creaking

wheels turned his head. A sorry wagon had just turned onto the street, and Nellie and Lady laboriously pulled it.

A catch was in Cassie's voice. "It's your family."

He nodded without speaking. The wagon was piled high with the family's meager possessions. Maw and Paw were on the front seat, and Hobe, Nobby, and Elodia rode behind them. A knot was in his throat. It wasn't hard to see that another family was leaving Montana.

The wagon stopped before them. Cassie reached for Ashel's hand. The pressure of her fingers told of the strain that was in her.

"Ashel," Paw said. "We're leaving. We're leaving this Godforsaken country. There's nothing here but fighting and starving."

Ashel remained silent. He could tell his father the fighting was over, but the starving depended upon the individual. Paw would not understand.

"We're going back to Missouri," Paw said. "Where a man's got a chance. You coming with us?"

Cassie's grip increased.

The knot in Ashel's throat grew. His mother was anxiously watching him, and Elodia said, "Come on, Ashel. We're going back home."

The word had no tug at him. He saw with a sudden clarity things would be no different for this family in Missouri—or anywhere else.

He shook his head. "No, I'm staying." He felt Cassie's grip loosen.

Elodia's eyes misted with tears, but she would recover. Kids recovered quickly.

His mother looked at Cassie, and her face dulled. "I

guess I knew that," she said.

Nobby said, "Who needs him? We'll get along."

Hobe groaned and shifted his injured leg.

Ashel knew how they would get along. He thought of the drab years ahead for his mother and Elodia. "Stay here," he said to his mother. "I'll take care of you and Elodia."

She placed her hand on Paw's arm. "He's my man," she said. A simple dignity firmed her face. "My place is where he goes."

Paw lifted the reins. "You got a chance to change your mind."

Ashel shook his head. Elodia wailed as Paw snapped the reins and yelled at Nellie and Lady. The wagon lumbered into motion and moved down the street. It was going to be a long, hard trip back to Missouri.

Ashel called after them, "Write to me, when you get settled."

He stared after the wagon, his throat constricted, his eyes stinging.

Cassie timidly touched his arm. "Did you want to go with them?"

"No." The harshness in his voice was not at her.

"I would've gone with you."

"No," he repeated. "We belong here." He looked at the distant mountains, their jagged pinnacles spearing the sky. There was no gentleness in this land. It relentlessly fought a man. It broke the weak and strengthened the strong. But a man accepted its fight and subdued it. He threw his silent challenge out into that vast emptiness.

He took her hand and said again, "We belong here, Cassie."

Center Point Publishing
600 Brooks Road ● PO Box 1
Thorndike ME 04986-0001 USA

(207) 568-3717

US & Canada:
1 800 929-9108